ALSO BY LAURA DALEO

Immortal Kiss

Bound by Blood

The Vampire Within

The Vow

The Soul Collector

The Doll

Once We Were Witches

MY NAME IS
Death

By

LAURA DALEO

AUTHOR LAURA DALEO

My Name is Death is a work of fiction. Names, characters, places, and incidents either are the product of the author's imagination or are used fictitiously. Any resemblance to actual persons living or dead, events, or locales is entirely coincidental.

Published in the United States by Author Laura Daleo, Tucson, Arizona

Print ISBN: 978-1-7366103-5-0

ebook ISBN: 978-1-7366103-4-3

"My Name is Death is a quick-paced story that kept me guessing the whole way through. If you like modern fantasy with suspense and strong emphasis on family, this has that in spades."

—Ariana, Gnomereader

"My Name is Death is a fascinating and compelling twist on the conception of the Angel of Death (or Death as he likes to be known), aka the Grim Reaper. Forget the image of the scary, robe-covered, sickle-carrying entity, Death dresses in Italian suits, velvet neckties, and oxford shoes. The story begins with Death on a holiday in New Orleans and encountering a terminally ill young lady, Annalise. Death knows that her time is limited, and he wants to help her to the afterlife. The two become friends in the short time they have together. God wishes that angels and humans could coexist in peace and learn from each other. One of God's other sons disagrees with this plan, believing angels are far superior than humans. The destruction begins, and only God can determine the outcome. This was a complete and utter surprise to me. The author composed a story of unexpected and fascinating twists on the conception of the Grim Reaper. The characters were well-written, and the plot was gripping from the first page, with all the elements of suspense, tension, action, and romance to keep the reader glued to the pages."

—Roger, BOOKLounge reviewer

"Take a dance with the angel of Death in this riveting story of immortals! Daleo keeps you guessing, and on your toes with anticipation in My Name is Death!"

—Elaina, Nook Nerds

Chapter 1

Nothing in life is certain except death and taxes. I hold this statement in high regard. Why? There are two possibilities. I could be a tax accountant—borrrinng—or I could be Death. If you guessed the latter, advance to go and collect $200. My name can influence anyone in a room; some say Grim Reaper, others say Angel of Death. I like to call myself Death. It has a pleasant ring and a powerful effect on people. The way "Death" embodies the style and pizazz of my attire, which includes Armani suits, ties, and shoes, influenced my decision to select it as my name. It had never occurred to me to dress in a dark robe, to carry a scythe or an hourglass, or to assume a skeleton physique.

The act of collecting and sending human souls into the afterlife is intimate, personal, and emotional. It is not a quick swipe of a weapon or an instrument to gauge time. Instead, it is a touch, an embrace, or a kiss that draws out the human soul and sends it on its journey beyond the Earth. As one might say, it's a date with Death.

I have kissed countless lips and released countless souls, but even Death has to take a holiday. There is no better place than New Orleans to take such a break. It has always been one of my favorite destinations. I'd fallen in love with the buzz of the city's historic heart, the French Quarter. Jackson Square fortunetellers come alive at dusk, and St. Louis Cathedral's windows reflect the fiery sunset. On Bourbon Street, neon signs flash in the night while jazz music blares in the background.

During this particular holiday, my hotel was in the heart of the French Quarter, steps from the Mississippi River. The room was quaint, decorated with warm tones and simple furnishings. A croissant and a cup of coffee were the perfect pairing on the cast-iron balcony as carriages passed by and ships sailed down the river. I couldn't ignore the aromas and noises emanating from the French Quarter situated directly beneath my room.

A floor-length mirror offered me a chance to evaluate my reflection before venturing onto the crowded street. What a handsome man I was, looking rather dashing in an Italian suit, a velvet necktie, and polished leather Oxfords. I had meticulously styled my short, dark-brown hair and scented my clean-shaven face with the finest cologne. I swiftly adjusted my tie, pocket square, and cufflinks, and I was ready to proceed.

With its brilliant rays, the sun reached out and greeted me. I shoved my hands in my pockets, strolling along the sidewalk, admiring the colorful historic buildings of the French Quarter, just a short distance from my preferred bench for people-watching. The rich, smoky aroma of coffee halted my progress and guided me straight into the Old Haven Coffee Bar.

After drinking an Americano, I continued on my way. Several feet between me and the bench, the familiar odor of disease roused my senses. Although I was on holiday, I could not ignore the source of the stench: a girl, perhaps 16 or 17 years old, slumped against the bench—my bench. Goosebumps scurried down my arms as I stared at her. She wore a thick wool sweater coat over a hospital gown, and dog-faced slippers covered her feet. Intrigue gripped me to my core. Rather than lying in a hospital bed waiting for Death to strike, she was sitting on *my* bench. I had to find out what had happened to her.

With my head held high, I approached her in my normal, confident manner. I unbuttoned my jacket, sat on the opposite end of the bench, and dipped my head in her direction. The disease raging inside her rushed up my nostrils and spun my head. Nothing short of a miracle could save her. She turned toward me and squinted, but not from the sun. The sarcastic look deepened as she puckered her dry, cracked lips, studying me with a scowl.

"You look too perfect to be real," she remarked.

A frown stretched across my forehead. "What do you mean by that?" I asked.

She flapped her hand in my direction and enlightened me. "You're not natural looking, with all your fancy clothing, gorgeous hair, and flawless complexion." She pushed herself upright and turned to face me. "And your eyes are too light. Nobody has eyes that color."

"Well, I do."

Several seconds passed before she seized my arm and pinched it.

Infuriated, I yanked my arm away. "Why on earth would you do something like that?"

"My pain causes me to hallucinate." She heaved a sigh. "I had to make sure that you were real."

"I assure you, I am very real." I exhaled an annoyed breath and second-guessed my decision to engage her.

Her sage-green eyes followed me, a sad smile tugging at the corners of her mouth. "I'm sorry. I'm not normally like that. It's just..." She gasped and doubled over, clutching at her stomach and blowing out quick, shallow breaths.

I scooted closer to her and put my hand on her shoulder. "Are you okay?"

"Give me a minute."

With every breath, she struggled, but I comforted her, "The pain will pass."

The cords in her neck relaxed, and she flopped backward against the bench. "I hate my life," she muttered. "I live in a box. My parents homeschool me. I have no friends—never had a boyfriend. My parents' house and the hospital are all I know."

Rather than say anything, I just waited, knowing more would follow.

A visible shiver echoed throughout her body as she lowered her gaze. "I have a rare autoimmune disease," she admitted. "My own immune system attacks itself. I live in a bubble because I catch everything, and my parents refuse to give up. Even at 17, I feel like I have no control over my life." Her hands trembled as she tucked them inside her sweater coat. "I don't understand why they cannot see my suffering. If I were a dog, they would have peacefully let me die a long time ago."

Trying to soothe her, I asked, "When did your disease begin?"

"I was born with it. I take painkillers and anti-inflammatory and immunosuppressant drugs. I've had dozens of plasma exchanges and intravenous immune therapy, but nothing helps," she said with tears welling up in her eyes.

"And your family does not see that?"

With a shrug, she flipped her long brown hair over her shoulders. "Maybe, I don't know. Maybe they just see what they want to see."

It was a scenario I had witnessed numerous times—family members who refuse to let go despite the suffering of their loved ones. A compassionate and strong person would have empathy for their loved ones had they walked in their shoes and experienced the pain they endured. Perhaps then they wouldn't stand in the way of the afterlife. That's where I came in. Only compelling logic and an understanding of when to release their souls are what I possess—no history, no emotion, no bias.

The girl's attire resurfaced in my mind, and I noticed the hospital gown peeking out from her sweater coat. "May I ask why you're wearing a hospital gown?"

Laughing, she added, "And my dog-faced slippers." It wasn't long before her joy faded. "I'm supposed to be in the hospital. I left my room and kept going. I didn't stop or look back. I took two buses, and when I got off, I turned around and walked the opposite way. So when they searched for me, they'd look in the wrong place."

Seeing how clever she was, I couldn't help but smile. She had bought herself more time. I squeezed her cold hand. "I'm impressed. As a self-advocate, I believe that people have the right to make their own health decisions. Of course, once they're old enough to understand the implications of their decisions. A 17-year-old is fully capable of handling this responsibility."

"I wish my parents saw it that way."

In response to her comment, I shrugged. "Forget about your parents. They aren't here, and you are. It's the French Quarter. Look around you. Historic charm abounds. The sky is clear, the sun is shining, and people are bustling about. Right?"

"Right."

I furrowed my eyebrows at her. "However, you look conspicuous in that hospital gown." I pulled out my money clip and handed her three hundred dollars. "There's a clothing store across the street. Buy yourself a change of clothing."

With her hands raised, she shook her head in disbelief. "I can't take your money."

"Yes, you can." I told her as I put the money in her hand.

"I have no means of paying you back."

"As you, I have no friends. It's just me; therefore, I have a lot of money. More than I can spend."

Silently, she gazed at her clenched fist, with a hint of green visible between her fingers. "It does not feel right," she said, looking up at me.

"I'm giving you a gift. Have you ever received one before?"

"Only from my parents."

"Go to the store and buy something that represents you because this ensemble certainly doesn't," I said, gesturing toward her entire outfit.

A giggle escaped her lips as she pushed herself to her feet. "I'll accept as long as it follows one condition."

"Which is?"

"Don't leave. Promise me you'll wait for me to return." Her eyes begged. "Please."

The fact that she assumed I would leave baffled me. She, however, did not know my true identity or why I had engaged with her in the first place. I crossed my finger over my heart and said, "I promise."

In that moment, she left, and I was alone. Solitude allowed me to gather my thoughts. She had not actually said the words, "I want to die." She had only mentioned the passing of a dog. The sad truth was, she reeked of death. Of course, it was not recognizable to a human, but I was Death, and hers was inevitable.

Chapter 2

She exited the store wearing baggy cargo jeans, a graphic retro T-shirt of butterflies, and platform sneakers. She draped the sweater coat over her arm. It seems odd that she would keep that thing. Apparently, she has some unknown reason for remaining attached to the article of clothing.

Standing before me, she curtsied, and a big smile spread across her face. "Is that better?" she asked.

"Yes, very much. Are you hungry? Would you like something to eat?"

Putting her hand on her stomach, she stated, "I might not be able to keep the food down."

"I see. Could we have something to drink, or is that out of the question as well?"

"Alcoholic beverages?"

"Nice try, but no. How about a soda?"

"Fine," she said with a roll of her eyes.

I ignored the pouty performance as I rose from the bench. "Let's take a stroll and find a soda shop."

She giggled. "A stroll?"

In response, I balked. "What's wrong with stroll?"

"Dude, nobody says that."

"My name is not Dude. Stroll simply means to walk."

She swatted my arm. "I know what it means, but the word isn't hip. You look like you're in your twenties, but you talk like you're a hundred years old. By the way, what's your name? I'm Annalise."

I bobbed my head in acknowledgment. "Ah, got it. I'll try to work on my coolness." I pursed my lips as I pondered telling her my name.

"What, you don't have a name?"

While we zigzagged down the crowded sidewalk, I avoided eye contact with her. Instead, I gazed at the vibrant buildings and greenery spilling out from balconies. The trot of horse hooves rang in my left ear, and I glanced in their direction. The carriage was full of drunken people toasting their glasses and singing off-key. Her persistent, inquisitive gaze compelled me to respond.

"Yes, I do, but it's complicated." I glanced at her. "It will only lead to questions. Once we have our soda, we'll find a place to sit and talk."

"Nothing like being all mysterious."

I dismissed her sarcasm. "You'd think one of these stores would have soda."

"I hope it isn't far," she said, clutching her stomach.

I studied the lines etched into her brow. "Are you in pain again?"

Rather than speaking, she nodded.

After forcing her to stop, I placed my hands on her shoulders. I lowered my head to match her eye level. "Look at me."

She obeyed.

As I locked eyes with her, I used my gift—not enough to kill her, but enough to block her brain's communication. In one blink, I altered her perception of pain. She swayed, and her eyes rolled back into her head for a moment before I released her. "Do you feel better now?"

A slow smile crossed her lips, and she laughed out loud. "God, yes. What did you do? No, wait. How did you do it?" She inquired, her eyes widening and darting about in confusion.

"I will explain once we find a quiet spot to talk." Taking my eyes off of her, I noticed the *Sip A Froth* sign swaying in the warm breeze. "That might be what we're looking for."

She turned her head in the direction I had indicated. "Either that, or it's a bar, and bars still serve soda."

"Indeed, they do."

As we entered the store, an explosion of colors greeted us. Candy, cookies, salty snacks, hats, sunglasses, mugs, postcards, and T-shirts crowded the small store. The entire back wall featured a massive soda selection, and Annalise rushed straight for it. She held up a bottle as I approached her. "Oh my God, Peanut Butter and Jelly soda!" she exclaimed.

"Sounds unpleasant."

She laughed out loud. "How about this one? Gross Gus Pimple Pop!"

Curling my lips, I cringed. "Hideous." I searched the shelves for something normal. "These will do."

"Frostie Root Beer and King Kong Cola? You're no fun."

"Your stomach will thank me."

She waved me away as she rummaged through the store. A high-pitched squeal pierced my eardrums. She ran toward me wearing a lace cloche hat and gold flower sunglasses. She waved a fedora hat and pineapple sunglasses at me. "Oh my God, put these on."

"What on earth for?"

"Come on. It will be fun, and the photo booth will help us capture our memories."

"Photo booth?"

"Yes, it's at the back of the store." She grabbed my arm and pulled me forward.

My gift had adversely affected her. She was high as a kite. I removed her hand from my arm and pointed to the counter. "Let me buy these first."

As I brought the fedora hat and pineapple monstrosities to the counter, she pointed to the hat on her head and sunglasses covering her eyes. "These too." She said with a bounce in her step.

The female clerk announced monotonously, "That's $83.97."

"Oh, and do you have a seating area where we can quench our thirst?" I inquired after handing her a hundred-dollar bill.

Annalise groaned and rolled her eyes. "We need to work on your vocabulary."

Instead, I turned my attention to the clerk behind the counter. She was clearly bored, as she twirled her finger around a strand of hair. "We do. You go around to the back and take the stairs up to the roof."

"Thank you."

"It's time to take pictures. Let's go!"

I sighed. "Very well."

After dragging me to the back of the store, she stopped in front of a tall wooden box with the words "PHOTO BOOTH" boldly written over the entrance. A round black stool sat in the center, facing a computerized screen with a camera located behind it. The opening was lined with red velvet curtains that I presumed could be drawn to provide privacy.

"Come inside," she beckoned to me after entering the contraption and sitting on one side of the stool. She patted the leather top and waved me forward, laughing blissfully.

"Now what?" I inquired as I sat on the opposite side of the stool, facing her.

"Okay, first we'll do a blissed-out smile with our hats and glasses. Then, we'll do a normal smile without glasses, then blow a kiss at the camera, and finally, a serious expression. Got it?"

As I pursed my lips and gathered my brows, I said, "Explain your blissed-out smile to me."

"Like this." She curved her lips, smiling ear-to-ear, and thrust her hands into the air.

In all of my existence, I had never displayed a blissed-out anything. "I'm not sure I'll be able to master this expression."

More laughter escaped her mouth as she said, "You'll be fine. Follow my lead. Oh, and we'll do two sets: one for each of us, so we'll have this memory to cherish."

"Shall we begin?" I smiled, despite not sharing her enthusiasm. She needed this day more than I did.

"Yes, please!"

As soon as I inserted a five-dollar bill, the machine began to hum, and a red light appeared in the center. Annalise shouted, "Blissed-out pose!"

It flashed brightly, and then the red light returned. Annalise threw her sunglasses aside and did the same for mine. "Okay, normal smile." She barely got the words out before the camera flashed. I wasn't sure whether I smiled or not before the red light appeared again. She hooked her arm loosely around my shoulders, puckered her lips, and mumbled, "Blow a kiss."

I was capable of doing that and blew an impressive kiss at the camera.

"The last one," she said, "serious face, and then we'll start over."

I could also effortlessly master this expression.

When the sessions ended, we waited outside the photo booth for our pictures to slide into a pocket. She bounced back and forth on her feet, her eyes fixed on the pocket. I couldn't comprehend the excitement. Immediately after the machine made a whirring noise, two photo strips shot into the pocket. When she saw them, she jumped and gasped out loud. "Oh, I love them!" she said, handing me one of the photo strips. "Look. They turned out so good!"

Upon seeing the four images, I bobbed my head in approval. The poses we struck were authentic and pleasing to the eye. She looked stunning, and I looked dashing.

"This is the best day of my life. Thank you!" she cried as she wrapped her arms tightly around my neck.

I smiled warmly at her. "You're very welcome. Shall we go upstairs to drink our sodas and talk?"

"Yes, absolutely."

As I gestured toward the front door, I said, "After you."

The clerk glanced up from her phone as we passed. There was something about Annalise that caught her attention. Taking a quick glance at her phone, the clerk fixed her wide-eyed gaze on Annalise. Although I had no proof, I assumed an Amber Alert had been issued; therefore, time was running out.

Chapter 3

Overgrown ivy vines covered a large pergola, serving as the centerpiece of the rooftop seating area. Creating a jungle atmosphere, the ivy vines spiraled down intricate columns of wrought iron and spilled onto the brick floor. White linen tablecloths were draped over black metal tables with matching chairs, while palm trees stood in the patio's corners. As we needed privacy in our conversation, I chose a table in the back left corner.

Annalise chose the chair facing the wall and popped open her soda. I pulled my chair closer to hers and placed my soda on the table. As I stared at her, reading her eyes, I contemplated how to begin my story.

"So, what's your name?"

"It is imperative that you have an open mind before I reveal my name."

She pressed her fingers against the sides of her head and then let them fly. "My mind is open."

"I'm serious. Believe me when I say you're unprepared for this information."

"Since you don't know me, you don't know what I can and can't handle."

"Very well, I'll get straight to it. I'm not human." I paused to emphasize the point. "My name is Death."

She pulled off her sunglasses and leaned over the table, staring. After a moment, she whispered, "Did you escape from a hospital too?"

I smirked and assured her that I hadn't done so. "No, I can tell from your expression that you don't believe me."

"Well, I mean. Come on."

"Did I not take away your pain?"

Her eyes flicked upward as her head tilted to one side. "Yeah, completely. I don't feel sick at all. I feel...normal. How did you do that anyway?"

In my confession, a sense of calm and ease flowed through me. "I have a gift—a special gift. My mission is to end people's suffering, their pain, and set their soul free. I have merely numbed your pain, but it will return."

Pressing her fist against her chest, she trembled. "So this gift—this euphoric feeling—you did this to me?"

"Yes."

"And it's temporary?"

"Yes."

She bit her lower lip. "So I'm not cured?"

"No."

"Am I still sick?"

My heart ached as I replied, "Yes." Her dull, empty eyes begged me. I had seen that look countless times—the realization that a miracle would never come. Delivering dreadful news never got easier. If I could somehow be an angel of mercy and relieve their pain without death, that would be my greatest accomplishment. Alas, I could not. My purpose was to end life, not resurrect it. Death was their only hope.

"I knew you were too perfect to be real—I mean human." Her gaze met mine before settling on the floor. "Are you like the Grim Reaper?"

"Some say Grim Reaper. Some say Angel of Death."

She slowly nodded. Was she trying to make sense of the existence of such an entity? Finally, she asked, "Did you come for me?"

"No," I replied quickly. "I'm on holiday, visiting the French Quarter. I happened upon you sitting on my favorite bench."

"Maybe it was fate." A pained look obscured her beauty. "To be honest, I'm not entirely sure I believe you. I mean, it's a lot." Holding her head between her palms, she elaborated on her point, "I can't comprehend that Death is a real person, let alone a handsome guy wearing an expensive suit."

"I sensed your illness and could have continued on my way, but your hospital gown, covered by that awful sweater coat, intrigued me." I reached for her hand and held it between mine. "I'm glad I stopped. You are most intriguing, Annalise."

She looked up at me, her sage-green eyes brightening. "I would be very disappointed if I suddenly woke up to find all of this a dream."

I pinched her arm.

"Ouch! Why did you do that?"

"For the same reason you pinched me. I'm real. You're real. This isn't a dream."

"Fair enough."

I furrowed my brow as I alerted her to the threat. "I believe your parents contacted the police and issued an Amber Alert."

"God, not again," she sighed heavily.

"You've escaped from hospitals before?"

She shouted, "Have you not been listening? I told you I've been sick my whole life!"

I kept my voice low as I said, "Calm down. I am listening. I heard everything you said. I'm not blaming you. I just want to figure out how long we have before the police arrive." I gestured toward her sunglasses. "Put those back on. They disguise your face. We benefit from your plain clothes and those glasses. That hospital gown would have attracted a lot of attention."

"I'm sorry. I hate not being in control of my life."

"When will you be 18?"

"Eight months."

It was not a lot of time; however, her impatience couldn't wait eight days, let alone eight months, and frankly, neither could her body. All her pain stemmed from her deteriorating liver. All she had to do was ask me, and I would promptly send her on her way. "Ah, I see."

"Usually, they find me right away and take me back to the hospital." She breathed a deep, long sigh. "Maybe my fake bus trip fooled them."

"Yes, that was clever."

"Well, I have had plenty of practice."

As I lifted my soda bottle, I said, "A toast to cleverness."

"Yes," she said, tapping hers against mine.

In a hushed voice, she asked, "So how did you become Death? Is it a job you applied for? Did you choose it?"

As memories stirred inside my brain, my breathing slowed. My thoughts traveled back to my earliest memory as I closed my eyes. There was no birth or creation that I could recall. The 19th century was the farthest back I could recall, or perhaps others before me had embodied Death. I had evolved over time, changing with the centuries. I glanced at the Italian suit I was wearing. In the past, my attire was not always modern. In those days, men wore coats, waistcoats, breeches, and white stockings. A chuckle escaped my lips. The styles of the 21st century were more appealing to me.

"Hello, earth to Death. Did you hear me?"

My focus returned to her after I shook off my thoughts. "Yes, I heard you. I have lived for a very long time. However, I cannot recall my birth. I believe I was chosen, but I have no evidence of this. What I am certain of is my purpose and responsibility to mankind."

As she spoke, more questions came. "Is it difficult to let people go? Is saying goodbye lonely? What if they're not ready to let go?"

"Well, that was quite a bit." I tapped my chin. "Let me respond. No, it's not difficult for me. I end their suffering. I offer them peace. I'm too busy with people every day to be lonely. I simply wait until they are ready."

"Are you happy?"

Coldness hit me like a punch in the gut. Was I happy? I had never considered whether I was happy or not. Family, friends, and lovers meant nothing to me. I had a purpose. I never deviated from that purpose. I looked her in the eyes and said, "I know my place. I'm content with who I am."

With a sad smile, her sage-green eyes seemed to glimpse into my soul. "What about today? Are you having a good time?"

As I gazed at her, I smiled. "I must admit that I am."

The sadness in her eyes vanished, and her cheeks turned a beautiful shade of pink. She finished her soda and set it on the table, then sighed deeply. "I'd like to just sit on the bench, bask in the sun, and observe people. That's until they find me."

"Is it your wish to be alone?"

"No, I'd rather have your company," she replied with a relaxed smile.

"It is a lovely bench and perfect for relaxing in the sun and people watching—two of my favorite things."

"Then we have something in common."

"Yes."

Chapter 4

As sunset approached, brushstrokes of saffron, lavender, rose, and gold dotted the darkening blue sky, painting a beautiful landscape as we sat together on the bench. A multitude of people meandered along the sidewalk, stopping to listen to jazz-funk electrified sounds of saxophones, trumpets, trombones, and drums. Tapping my foot to the beat and closing my eyes, I became one with the instruments.

The sound of Annalise's soft humming caught my attention. In a side-to-side motion, she swayed her head with her fingers drumming against her thighs. The costume sunglasses were lying beside her, no longer covering her face. I glanced into the crowd, noticing how many people were staring at her and checking their phones. I guessed a police visit would be forthcoming. As she grooved to the music, I interrupted her, saying, "You asked me if I was happy. How about you?"

A radiant smile swept across her face as she replied, "In this particular moment, I'm very happy."

"And today, you are free."

"Yes. Today is a good day."

"Before today?"

Her shoulders slumped as she bowed her head and answered in a quiet voice, "Maybe when I was a child and couldn't comprehend my illness. When I got older and my disease progressed, joy vanished from my vocabulary. My pain and being trapped in a bubble have destroyed me." Despite all the trauma she had experienced, she smiled at me and said, "But, Death, or whoever you are, you gave me the best day of my life, and I will be forever grateful."

"I've told you the truth. I am Death, just as I said I was. If you require evidence, I can confirm that the pain has returned. You should feel it any moment now."

She snorted with laughter. "Yeah, right. I feel fin…" She gasped for breath, hunching over. "Why would you do this?" she demanded, tears welling up in her eyes. "For the sake of proving yourself? How cruel of you."

My response was firm. "Of course not. I wouldn't cause anyone pain. It was my gift that removed your pain, but it wasn't permanent. I cannot cure you. I only knew when your pain would return."

Her head flopped backward, and a mournful cry escaped her mouth. "I can't go through this any longer. Take my pain away again, please!"

"I want you to look at me."

She stared at me with her feverish, overbright eyes, pleading.

I blocked the vile dark matter gnawing away at her liver once more. She let out a huge breath, sagged against me, and threw her limp arms around my neck. "Thank you," she whispered.

As I cupped her face in my hands, I forced her to look at me. "I am happy to help. You only have to ask."

With tears streaming down her cheeks, she said, "I believe you. I'm sorry I doubted you."

"We must focus on the future. I'm certain many people have noticed you. The arrival of the police is inevitable."

"I had figured as much. There's no way I can keep running. Today was wonderful for me. I will never forget it."

"Do you have anything you want to accomplish that you haven't yet done? There's no better moment than the present."

Gazing out into the street, she paused to observe the jazz musicians performing outside a bar. "Do you dance?" she asked.

"What?"

As she turned to me, she said, "Y'know, dancing, like moving to the beat."

My only dancing experiences were at a wedding, a gala, and a reunion. Despite my poor dancing skills, each occasion required my presence to send someone's soul into the afterlife. "I'm certainly not a talented dancer, but yes, I have."

"It would mean everything to me to dance in front of a live band. I've only danced alone in my bedroom."

Once she saw my dance moves, I wasn't sure she'd feel the same way. In spite of this, her freedom was about to expire, and she hadn't asked to move on to the afterlife. Surely, I couldn't deny her a couple of dances. As I rose, I extended my hand. "Very well."

A warm glow lit up her eyes as she tapped her heart with a loose fist. "You're all right, Death. I kinda like you."

"Having compassion is something that I value highly, Annalise."

"There you go again," she said, rolling her eyes at me.

"What?"

"Your vocabulary. I complimented you. Accept it with a smile and move on." She waved me away and said, "Whatever, let's dance."

As she bounced off the bench, she grabbed my hand and dragged me to the lively mortals dancing in the middle of the street. When she hit the makeshift dance floor, she began to move her body in time with the beat. I stood helplessly beside her, trying to dance while my body rocked back and forth.

"Boogie down!" she exclaimed, glancing up at me with an infectious smile.

Getting into the groove, I thrust my hands in the air and swayed my hips while shouting, "Yeah!"

Everything else faded into the background as we lost ourselves in the music and vibrant atmosphere.

Several upbeat songs later, I'd stripped off my jacket and loosened my tie. The hot weather, limited breeze, and the fact that I was dancing like a fool had me drenched in sweat. She danced nonstop, drunk on my gift, but she was happy, and that's all that mattered.

After the band switched gears, smooth jazz serenaded the crowd. Annalise and I stared at each other in silence. She narrowed the gap between us as she said, "I will never be able to go to the prom or a school dance. I have a slim chance of ever experiencing any of those events. You don't owe me anything, but tonight is probably my last chance to slow dance with a boy." She put out her hands and asked, "Can we dance together?"

The responsibility of sending a soul into the afterlife was always intimate, personal, and emotional. However, she wanted a dance that would be remembered forever. I was on holiday when I met her. I felt compelled to end her suffering, please her, and satisfy her every whim. To me, she was a bird with a broken wing, and I was the healer. "Of course, I will."

She looked into my eyes and whispered, "Thank you."

I wrapped my arm around her waist and reached for her opposite hand. The two of us swayed back and forth, our feet moving in a circle. I looked at her for a moment, but her eyes never left mine. A flicker of gold in the background caught my attention. I spotted them immediately. Four police officers approached us, followed by a man and a woman huddled together, their expressions angst-ridden. I whispered in Annalise's ear, "The police are here, and I think your parents are too."

After breaking free from me, she trembled uncontrollably and turned around to face the crowd. "No," she cried.

One of the four officers raised his hands in a nonconfrontational gesture as he said, "Annalise, we're here to help."

It took only a few seconds for people to scatter, leaving Annalise and me on display.

The woman with the same brown hair as Annalise shrieked loudly. "Annalise! Thank God. Honey, we were sick with worry."

"Come to us, Annalise." The man motioned toward himself. It was evident from his graying hair and bloodshot eyes that her disease had taken a heavy toll on him.

"No. I won't! Stay back!"

The officer's gaze shifted to me. "Sir, step away from her," he said while pushing his hands downward. "Please don't interfere. This is a private matter."

"Don't blame this on him," Annalise shouted back at them as she pointed to herself. "I ran away. He has no involvement in this."

"Please, Annalise. Don't make this harder than it has to be."

"I won't go back. I won't." Her body trembled violently, and she clenched her fists. "I'm suffering. I'm dying. Mom, Dad, you need to let me go."

"Don't say that," her mother clasped her hands and pleaded. "The doctors say there's hope. We need to keep fighting."

Her father echoed her mother's words. "Yes, Baby. We can beat this."

The blood drained from Annalise's hands as she stood completely still. "Okay. Just let me say goodbye to my friend."

"Take your time, Baby."

She turned around and faced me. A somber expression distorted her tear-soaked face. "You stated that all I needed to do was ask. Well, here I am asking. Please end my suffering and free my soul."

"Yes, Annalise, of course." I pulled her into my embrace and laid my lips over hers, unleashing my gift's fatality. With vengeance, it streamed into her mouth, shutting down her heart, brain, and lungs. My gift simultaneously freed and killed her, leaving me transfixed by her lifeless eyes.

As her body fell limp in my arms, her soul flew into the heavens and healed her broken wings. In front of the police and her parents, it was my responsibility to deliver a performance. I sobbed in agony as I cradled her in my arms. "Help!" I screamed. "Something's wrong. She just collapsed and isn't breathing."

Police rushed forward, her parents seconds behind. They shoved me out of the way and huddled around her. "She has no pulse." The policeman glanced at his partner next to him and said, "Call it in. I am starting CPR."

Her mother screamed out, "Noooo!" and fell to her knees.

Her father knelt by her, wrapping his arms around her, his chin trembling uncontrollably as he struggled to hold it together. As I watched them perform CPR over and over, I knew her heart would never beat again. They couldn't save her.

Within 10 minutes of arriving at the scene, paramedics connected her to a monitor and continued CPR. They checked her pulse and breathing every few minutes. During the course of CPR, a straight line ran across the screen, confirming what I already knew. "She is in asystole," the paramedic said after several attempts.

Her mother screamed, "Do something!"

"There's nothing we can do," the paramedic said.

Chapter 5

Following everyone's departure, the French Quarter fell into a dead calm. I remained seated in the chair where I had hung my jacket, holding onto the photo strip of Annalise and me. I had released the bubbly girl, wearing outrageous sunglasses and beaming with joy, into the afterlife. For the first time in my existence, sorrow crept into my heart, and I felt completely alone. My thoughts flashed back to her sassy, impatient, and animated nature, as well as the vividness of her eyes after receiving a small portion of my gift. Out of all the souls I had released, none affected me like her.

I had experienced this type of intimacy with others many times before. It wasn't the first time I had to personally interact with the lives of the souls I released, nor would it be the last. It was my privilege to accompany them on their last shopping spree, have a final meal with them, and listen to their concerns during a conversation. Although I knew what it was like to grieve the passing of a loved one, I did not love Annalise. I barely knew her, but Annalise had left a lasting impression on me. Why had she had such an impact on me?

My fingers pressed against my temples and massaged my aching brain before I slowly stood up from the chair. As I dragged my feet along the sidewalk toward my hotel room, I lowered my head and gazed toward the ground. Locking myself inside the room, I hung the "do not disturb" sign on the outside of the door. The room was dark, but I preferred it. I sank into the chair tucked into the corner and left the lights off. Staring off into the distance, I became inert, with no thoughts, emotions, or feelings—just a hollow shell. Annalise changed everything for me. I stayed in the chair for the entire night, unwilling to move.

Throughout the course of four days, I remained frozen in my melancholy state, only getting up to use the bathroom or drink water. As I hadn't removed the "do not disturb" sign from my door, the hotel manager called to check on me. I assured them I was fine, and they would have access to my room by tomorrow.

That fourth day, a bright beam of sunlight penetrated the room through the slats of the shutters. Mentally numb, I pushed myself out of the chair and into the shower. As I soaked my body in cold water, I shook off the drowsiness and mixed in hot water. Following my normal routine, I showered, shaved, groomed my hair to perfection, and slipped into a clean suit. As I stared in the floor-length mirror, my usual spark waned, like a pilot light without its flame. I brushed off the feeling and proceeded out the door.

Once again, I stopped at the Old Haven Coffee Bar. After the first sip, I no longer desired my Americano. To avoid hurting the clerk's feelings, I took it to go. On my way to my bench, I threw the cup in the trash, again brushing off the difference in my behavior. I sighed with relief as my bench emerged, vacant. Now that I had it all to myself, I could relax and enjoy some peace. I sat near the middle with my arms wrapped around the back of the bench. The streets were filled with people conversing, chattering away on their phones, sightseeing, and appearing to be enjoying themselves. A deep, weighty sigh accompanied my realization that I was alone. Even my bench no longer appealed to me.

As I closed my eyes, I leaned my head back against the bench. "Hey, you."

My heart raced as I thought, "Now I am hearing her voice in my head."

"Death, it's me, Annalise."

In a panic, I curled my arms around my body and held on tightly. What had happened to me? Had I lost my mind? Had I gone insane? A sharp pinch sent tingles down my arm. My eyes widened to see Annalise's ethereal sage-green eyes. I squeezed my eyes shut, rubbed them, and looked again.

"I'm still here." She shrugged. "Aren't you glad to see me?"

"No, no, no. You can't be here." I shook my head vigorously. "I've got to get my bearings."

"You're not seeing things. I'm really here."

I jerked my head toward the sound of approaching footsteps, desperate for a sanity check. Two men walked toward me, one younger, perhaps in his 20s, the other older, perhaps in his early 50s. Were they father and son? I was uncertain, and it didn't matter. I simply needed help. My voice trembled as I called out, "Excuse me."

Both men abruptly halted in front of me. "Yes," the older man replied.

As I pressed my lips together and swallowed hard, I kept my gaze on them. "I know this is going to sound crazy, but—"

"Take your time. It's okay."

"Um." I laughed nervously. "Is there a girl with long brown hair sitting next to me wearing a blue T-shirt and black jeans?"

The men glanced at each other, confirming my suspicions that I was losing my mind.

The older man stepped closer and said, "I have no idea what you're going through or why you'd ask that." He patted my shoulder and smiled, "but she's definitely sitting next to you."

In a whirl, I turned my head toward Annalise.

Gratitude filled her face as she said, "Thanks for helping. He's been through a lot lately, but he'll be fine."

"Glad we could help," he replied before they continued on their way.

I stared wide-eyed at her. "How can this be? I don't understand."

An inviting smile spread across her face. "I asked God for a favor."

"What?"

"I told him Death needed a friend."

"And he agreed to that?"

"I shared with him how you brought an end to my agony. You were the one who saved me. He admired you for that." The corners of her lips curled, widening her smile. "Getting me back to Earth, however, took some coaxing."

My stomach fluttered as I asked, "How long can you stay?"

Taking my hand, she said, "I'm here for good."

As I gawked at her with my mouth hanging open, my immortal heart seemed to freeze before pounding inside my chest. After several seconds, I found my voice. "So, like, forever," I blurted out.

She replied, "Yes," in her bubbly voice.

A smile came to my lips as I embraced her. A sudden thought struck me: how could others see her? After her death, she ascended to Heaven. As I pulled away, I held her at arm's length. "Are you an..."

Patting herself on the back, she said, "Yup. I earned my angel wings, and I'm your sidekick."

My frown deepened. "Sidekick."

"Yes, sir."

"I guess I could use some assistance."

"Also, I think we should give you a better name than Death."

"What's wrong with Death?"

"Death isn't a name." Her eyes grew large. "How about Clayton, or simply Clay?"

I tilted my head from side to side, pursing my lips. "I do like the name Clay."

"Clay, it is." She nudged my shoulder. "And your suit. It's too businessy. You'd look amazing in jeans and a T-shirt."

"This is an Armani suit. It's very expensive," I said while stroking the front of my jacket.

"Fine, but dress for the occasion. Sitting on a bench doesn't require a suit and tie, does it?"

"Fair enough." My gaze swept over her, noticing her sparkling eyes, glowing skin, lustrous hair, and happiness radiating from her. After saving her from all her suffering, I felt I had contributed to part of that bliss.

"You're staring," she said, gently nudging my shoulder once more.

"I missed you. I can't help it."

"I missed you too."

"I don't know why God sent you back to me. Maybe he felt pity for me. Maybe he thought I needed a guardian angel to watch over me. Whatever the reason," I placed my hand on my chest, "words cannot express my gratitude. My immortal heart is overflowing with emotions." My mouth grew dry, and a visible shakiness came over me.

Softly squeezing my hand, she assured me, "I'm not going anywhere."

"Promise me."

As she dipped her head to one side, a shy smile spread over her lips. "I promise."

As my gaze swept over her, her lips curled upward, broadening her smile. My gratitude for our connection was overwhelming at that moment. Her mesmerizing sage-green eyes reflected warmth and unwavering trust, like windows to her soul. It wasn't just her smile and eyes that comforted me, but rather her genuine kindness and understanding. "How do we proceed from here?" I asked.

She smirked and pointed to my clothing, just as I had initially done to her. "First of all, you look conspicuous in that suit." She gestured at me, saying, "It's too dressy for a park bench. There is a clothing store across the street. Get yourself something hipper."

"Haha. Very funny."

"I'm not kidding. Jeans and T-shirts are calling your name."

I pulled my eyebrows into a defiant scowl. "I'll look ridiculous."

Shaking her head, she said, "I guarantee you'll look dope."

It dawned on me as I gazed at her that she had only the clothes she was wearing. It was a must for her, whether I shopped or not. I rose from the bench and extended my hand to her. "God sent you to me with only clothes on your back. I believe this wardrobe mission should include you as well."

She giggled and grabbed my hand. "Let's do it."

Rows upon rows of clothing in various colors and styles greeted us as we entered the clothing store. I watched Annalise explore each aisle, choosing items that caught her eye for herself and me. She carried a flowery bohemian dress, an edgy leather jacket, a few pairs of pants, and several tops. My arms were full of jeans and T-shirts. I groaned, overwhelmed by all the options.

Annalise noticed my hesitation and narrowed down my choices. "Try these on. They're perfect."

"How do you know that? I'm always in a suit."

She grinned slyly. "I just know." She walked away, leaving me to ponder what she meant.

She returned moments later with stacks of accessories to complete our outfits: necklaces, funky hats, and even a pair of sunglasses that screamed "cool." As she handed the sunglasses to me, I couldn't help but notice the excitement in her eyes.

"Well, at least they aren't pineapple-shaped."

"Come out and show me each outfit," she said after shooing me into a dressing room.

When I stripped out of my suit, I shook my head. I loved my suits, so why was I doing this? For her. I did it for Annalise. In front of the mirror, I frowned. I stared back at myself like a stranger in this casual ensemble. The blue jeans were ripped and faded on purpose. The form-fitting white T-shirt caught my eye. While the outfit emphasized my muscular physique, it was a stark contrast to the tailored elegance I usually wore. As I adjusted the sunglasses, fluorescent lighting reflected off them. I couldn't deny that I looked like someone else, someone who belonged in a world far removed from my polished suits and sophisticated charm.

"Clay, what's taking so long?"

"I don't want to come out."

"Come on," she pleaded. "I want to see."

After taking off the sunglasses, I cracked the door and peeked out. My immortal heart fluttered. She looked stunning in the flowery bohemian dress. The vibrant colors of the dress complemented her infectious energy. Despite feeling self-conscious in my unfamiliar attire, seeing her happiness made it all worthwhile.

With rosy cheeks and a slight curve in her lip line, she waved me forward with anticipation.

Taking a deep breath, I stepped out of the dressing room. Annalise's eyes lit up as she took in my appearance. Her smile widening, she exclaimed, "You look incredible." Her praise temporarily swept away my initial doubts.

"You're sure?"

She playfully smacked my shoulder. "You look amazing."

"Those jeans will definitely turn heads," said a saleswoman walking by.

"See."

"She has to say things like that." I said, brushing it off.

"This isn't one of your precious suits, so you don't want to admit you look good."

Clad in my casual clothes, my confidence wavered as I stared into the three floor-length mirrors outside the dressing rooms. "Maybe. I just look so different."

She giggled as she approached me. "Being a cute guy in jeans isn't something you're used to. But seriously, they fit perfectly, and that shirt makes your eyes pop."

Standing there, I stared into her eyes. "Do these clothes really fit my style?"

With a wide smile, she nodded. "Trust me, you look hip and handsome."

Looking at my reflection in the mirror, Annalise's words resonated deeply with me, and I felt a surge of confidence. Had I unearthed a side of myself that formal clothing had obscured? "I'll add them all to my wardrobe. Did you find all you needed?"

As she answered, a spark of delight appeared in her eyes. "I did. Thank you."

Before heading back to my dressing room, I said, "It appears we are ready to proceed. After I change, I'll make our purchases."

We strolled down the street, enjoying the sun as we made our way to the hotel. Throughout the narrow streets, colorful balconies adorned with wrought iron railings and vibrant flowers were lined with fragrant jasmine. The terracotta roofs of these tall, narrow buildings gleamed in the afternoon sun. I couldn't help but smile, feeling warmth in my chest that wasn't just a result of the sun. As we walked, I realized just how much I had missed her presence, and I silently vowed to never let her slip away again.

Inside the hotel room, I set the shopping bags down on the floor in a corner. After surveying the quaint room with simple furnishings, Annalise fixed her gaze on me. Her brows furrowed. I could tell she was mulling over something. Her expression grew more determined with each passing second.

"Is there something wrong?" I asked.

"I'm just blurting this out because I don't know how else to ask. Do you have a home?"

I laughed as I admitted, "I don't need a house."

"So you live in hotels?"

"My life's mission is to help souls find peace. In every city I visit, I meet people who have unfinished business here on Earth. After releasing their souls, I carry their stories with me to the next place I travel to. So, yes, I do live in hotels."

Her expression changed from inquisitive to fascinated, but her questions persisted. "Do you have others who can help you?" Her tone was full of curiosity, as if she wanted to uncover more about the mystery of Death.

"I'm alone in this."

She blinked as a flash of uncertainty raced across her face. "The number of people dying must outweigh one person's ability to free them. Even just me and you...it's impossible."

I shrugged as I stood there. "My purpose is to send souls to God's Kingdom, though many people pass away without ever coming into contact with me."

Her fixation deepened as she rubbed her forehead. My comments only seemed to aggravate her, but how can one explain death? An intangible force guided me when someone's time was near, directing me to those whose souls I must free. There was an order to everything, an unexplainable balance. Taking her hands in my own, I said, "It is a mysterious process that I cannot fully comprehend. It is as if an unseen hand is guiding me. It gives me solace to know that, though I may be alone in my mission, I am a part of a much greater plan."

"I was just a sick girl. Why did my soul ascend to Heaven? I never set foot inside a church or had a religious background."

I gently squeezed her hands as I explained, "Religious beliefs or church attendance do not solely determine the path to Heaven. The purity of one's soul and the lessons learned throughout one's lifetime guide this journey."

"But how?"

I stumbled for the right words, pondering the importance of the question, eventually saying, "Only God knows that answer."

Chapter 6

Eight months ago, God sent Annalise back to me, who celebrates her birthday today. I'm determined to make this day as special as possible, even though I am not hosting her party. "Annalise, it's your eighteenth birthday. I should be taking you out to an intimate dinner, but instead, Alan is hosting a birthday gala for you. By the way, without my gift, Alan wouldn't be alive. His heart has survived five months longer than it otherwise would have. This is not the intent of my gift. I cannot continue prolonging his death. Alan's manipulative games must stop."

After looking at me for a moment, she glanced back at the bathroom vanity mirror and twisted a section of her hair around the barrel of a curling iron. "He's an old man who has no one and just wants to please us." She released the curl from the iron carefully, creating a gorgeous, bouncy ringlet.

"But at what cost?" I asked. "His bucket list cannot dictate our actions."

"We'll talk to him tonight after my party."

My gaze traveled around our recently redecorated master bedroom, taking in the cream-colored chairs by the fireplace, the stunning crystal chandelier, and finally admiring the wood-vaulted ceilings above our king-sized bed, which was surrounded by cream pillows. One of the walls opposite the bed had a large folding window that stretched the entire width of the room. A magical aura filled the deck as stars twinkled over the mountain peaks. Despite my reservations about Alan's motives, I could not ignore the beauty of our suite.

It brought back memories of buying the four-bedroom house in Yorba Linda, California. Annalise wanted a home, and I didn't hesitate to buy it for her. Over the past eight months, I'd fallen in love with her. To be honest, I think I fell in love with her the moment I saw her on my bench. Though I often wondered if she reciprocated my feelings, I did nothing to confirm if she did. While we shared a bedroom, we slept on opposite sides, never getting close to each other. My hope had been that she would declare her feelings with a glance, a touch, a few words, or some other gesture, but she had not.

I once again found myself in the present, staring at her as she gently arranged her curls. As I watched her eyes sparkle with excitement, I longed to understand the depth of her emotions—to know what she was really thinking.

"We'll have a wonderful time at the party, and we'll dance together again," she conveyed in one breath.

"I think the formal attire will go well with my slow dancing style," I pointed out.

She laughed and said, "And you're much better at that type of dancing."

"When we danced in the French Quarter, you seemed to like my dance moves."

Despite raising her eyebrows and smiling, she did not elaborate.

I pursed my lips and frowned. Was that look conveying a message? In my mind, I clearly remember her saying "boogie down" as she acknowledged my moves. However, I also recall she was high on my gift. That was in the past. Taking Alan's gala into consideration, I imagined an elegant ballroom filled with sparkling chandeliers. In our formal attire, she and I would glide along the dance floor, twirling in perfect harmony to the rhythm of a romantic waltz. Her 18th birthday would be a night to remember, and dancing with her again would also be a part of the celebration. This time around, I'd make sure she was impressed.

After rising from the vanity seat, Annalise entered her walk-in closet. We each had our own, which included a seating area next to a floor mirror, surrounded by built-ins. I draped my black tuxedo jacket over my closet chair and slipped into my pleated white shirt. Inside the pocket of my jacket sat Annalise's birthday gift. I decided that now was the perfect time to give it to her.

In my excitement, I cleared my throat before stepping into her space. As I pulled out the small velvet box, her eyes widened with anticipation. The soft light danced off the polished surface, enhancing the moment. "Happy birthday, Annalise," I said, my voice sincere.

She glanced at me before unwrapping the gift box. Inside, she found a delicate silver necklace with a pendant in the shape of a blooming flower, adorned with sparkling diamonds. Her breath caught in her throat; her mouth slackened. "Oh, it's beautiful." Her voice rose as she exclaimed, "I love it! It's the perfect birthday surprise." She handed the necklace to me before turning around and sweeping her hair to the side. "Can you fasten it for me, Clay?"

"Of course," I said, carefully hooking the clasp. The pendant rested against her smooth skin, its shimmering diamonds reflecting the light in a mesmerizing way. Delight ballooned inside my chest as my heartbeat quickened, knowing I had chosen a gift that captured her beauty and made her birthday celebration even more unforgettable.

"It complements my dress as if you chose it specially for it."

"I can't wait to see you in your gown."

"And I am looking forward to seeing you in your tux. We will be a perfect match with our black outfits."

Silence filled the room as we gazed at each other. In my head, I yelled, *Seize the moment; tell her. Tell her you love her. Don't procrastinate. Don't run through what-ifs. You're in the moment—that moment when everything else fades away as you fixate on each other. Tell her, you fool!*

As she shooed me away, she broke the spell. "Clay, finish getting ready. Alan will pick us up soon." She didn't wait for a reply as she disappeared behind the closed door. I wondered if I should follow her inside and do as my thoughts commanded and confess my love. A wave of uncertainty washed over me and shattered my confidence. *Was* it the right time? Would she feel the same way? What if my confession appalled her? I couldn't bear that!

I sighed and grabbed my jacket off the chair, its wool fabric smooth against my fingertips. As I buttoned up my shirt, I rehearsed my words. Deep down, I knew I could not let fear stop me from expressing my true feelings to Annalise; regardless of the outcome, she needed to know how I felt.

In the full-length mirror, I examined my finished appearance—a ritual I had always performed before going out. I adjusted the collar of my crisp white shirt, making sure it sat flat against my neck. With a touch of pomade, I smoothed my neatly styled hair, making sure it was perfectly in place. After a moment of reflection, I nodded at my appearance, but I was more interested in hearing her opinion than in what I thought. My goal was to impress Annalise.

Awaiting the unveiling of her gown, I paced back and forth in front of her closet door. After several minutes of pacing, the clicking of her heels on the wood floor approached the door. As it swung open and she emerged in the doorway, my eyes took in every inch of her. The strapless dress revealed her flawless décolletage, while the fitted bodice emphasized her small waist. The rich, black fabric cascaded down her body, pooling at her feet in an elegant sweep. The way it hugged her curves left me speechless. Annalise was right; the necklace complemented the dress beautifully. She looked effortlessly glamorous, and I couldn't stop staring. In adoration, I finally said, "You look absolutely stunning."

"And you look very handsome in your tailored suit," she said, her fingers lingering on my jacket. I couldn't help but smile as she delicately straightened the edges of my bow tie. The warmth of her touch sent a wave of excitement through me, making me feel giddy like a teenage boy. I was going to tell her. The moment was perfect.

The doorbell chime stopped me. A bright glow filled her eyes as she hurried to the front door. The confession of my love never left my lips, only a sigh, as I followed her. She couldn't contain her joy as she swung open the door. "Hello, Alan." She kissed his wrinkled cheek.

As he returned her kiss, his weathered and worn hands clasped hers. He looked dapper in a classic black tux. Alan neatly brushed his salt-and-pepper hair back from his aging face. Although he was old and struggling with heart disease, Alan stood tall and sophisticated. He patted me on the back as he reached out and hugged me. His frail body reminded me of the number of times I had given him my gift. Although my gift had extended his life, I was also aware that his time was running out.

He stepped aside and looked us both over. "What a lovely couple you are." He waved us forward. "Come. My driver is waiting."

As we stepped outside, a sleek black limousine awaited us, its doors opened by a sharply dressed chauffeur. The plush leather seats enveloped us as we settled in, and the soft lighting created a romantic atmosphere. The limousine glided through the city streets as Alan regaled us with stories of his youth, transporting us to an era of wealth and power. He recounted lavish vacations in private jets and weekends spent at their sprawling estate, complete with a staff of servants attending to their every need. Though we'd heard these stories many times, we listened intently.

****

We entered Alan's mansion through a grand foyer filled with travertine floors and crystal chandeliers. A majestic walnut staircase stood in the center of the foyer, surrounded by exquisite artwork that spoke of wealth and sophistication. The meticulous arrangement of fresh flowers in porcelain and gold vases filled the air with a delicate scent. The air of luxury that permeated everything from the velvet curtains to the elaborate antique furniture struck us as we walked through the foyer.

Violins, cellos, and trumpets reverberated off the mansion's walls. The music enveloped me, pulling at my emotions, leaving me vulnerable and energized. The music grew louder and more enchanting as we moved further into the mansion. Upon turning a corner, Alan's path led us to double doors with brass handles. The music came from behind the doors. He escorted us through them with a wave of his hand.

We entered a magical ballroom and walked under gold decorations cascading from the ceiling and spilling onto the floor. The mirrored walls reflected dazzling lights overhead. The harmonious instruments played by the orchestra set the stage for the celebration. The room was alive with laughter and conversation as guests dressed in formal attire strolled about. Every table featured glamorous floral arrangements, each of which made a bold statement with its vibrant colors and delicate blooms. I stared at Annalise, radiating beauty and happiness at her birthday gala. Her smile grew wider with each passing second.

Alan led us right up to the orchestra at the front of the room. The conductor silenced the musicians before handing Alan a microphone. A waitress brought a tray of glasses filled with sparkling champagne. Alan grabbed three glasses off the tray, offering us each a glass.

High-pitched feedback echoed through the mic as Alan said, "Hello." The sound crew quickly fixed the issue before giving Alan a thumbs up. Alan's voice echoed throughout the room, commanding everyone's attention. The crowd grew silent, their eyes fixed on him.

He angled his head in our direction as he said, "I'd like you to meet the guests of honor, Annalise and Clay, my friends. Without their support, I wouldn't have been able to survive my health issues. Tonight, we have a special event. In honor of Annalise's 18th birthday, I am hosting this gala."

The room erupted in applause, the sound echoing off the high ceilings. The crowd cheered as Alan continued, "There will be an open bar, appetizers, and cake for later." He pointed to a five-layered cake with royal blue icing and intricate white roses and pearls. "Annalise has brought light and joy into my life, so let us raise our glasses and toast her birthday."

As the crowd raised their glasses, the clinking of crystal filled the air. Annalise blushed under the spotlight as she looked out at the sea of smiling faces.

My hand rested on her lower back as I whispered, "I've got to hand it to Alan. What a magnificent birthday celebration he's given you."

She whispered back, "I'm overwhelmed."

The sight of her delight and the realization of Alan's gesture overwhelmed me too. I couldn't have asked for a better celebration for someone who brought so much happiness to my life.

"Grab some appetizers, dance, and enjoy yourselves!" Alan nudged us forward before leaving us behind. As he sat with his friends and his younger brother, his only living relative, the music filled the room with vivid sounds. It drew couples to the dance floor. Alan's eyes shined with contentment as he saw the joyous atmosphere he created for Annalise's special day.

As the spicy aroma of appetizers wafted through the air, my stomach growled. "Are you hungry?" I asked Annalise.

"I could eat a few bites."

The food and bar station featured an ice sculpture as its centerpiece in the far corner of the room. The appetizer spread was stunning, with a variety of bite-sized delicacies presented on silver platters. It was hard not to notice the colorful signature cocktails crafted by the bartenders as we made our way through the crowd.

"Oh my goodness. Try this," Annalise said into my right ear.

She popped a stuffed mushroom into my mouth. The warm, crispy breading gave way to a creamy, savory filling that exploded with flavors of garlic, cheese, and herbs. My taste buds danced in delight. Licking my lips, I proclaimed, "I must have more of these."

She piled more mushrooms on her plate, saying, "I know, right?"

She carefully chose each mushroom, as if creating a work of art on her plate. I couldn't resist joining her, adding appetizer after appetizer to my own plate, eager to indulge in the culinary delights.

We chose a small table tucked away in a corner. Against a white tablecloth, the floral arrangements on this table were especially vibrant. As I pulled out her chair, I noticed her full champagne glass. As the bubbles slowly rose to the top, untouched by her lips, I asked, "Would you like another drink? Perhaps a soda?"

"The champagne is too bitter," she said, pushing it aside. "But I didn't want to ruin Alan's toast. Soda would be perfect."

"One soda coming right up."

While at the bar, I browsed the soda menu. I brought back two refreshing glasses of fizzy cola. We sipped our sodas and munched on appetizers as lively chatter and laughter filled the air around us. Soft music echoed throughout the room, creating an inviting setting.

Annalise and I exchanged glances, struck by the perfect balance between taste and atmosphere.

After finishing the appetizers and taking a sip of soda, I noticed Alan approaching our table. "Hey there, you two! Having a wonderful time?" His voice boomed with enthusiasm. He leaned in and whispered, "Don't hide in the corner, my friends. This celebration is for both of you. Get up, feel the rhythm, and let the music guide your feet. Dance like nobody's watching!" With a mischievous smile, he twirled away, leaving us both staring at each other.

I reached my hand across the table and asked, "Would you like to dance?"

As Annalise considered my outstretched hand, a blush tinted her cheeks. "I have no idea what any of these dances are. I'll probably trip over you."

"Don't worry," I reassured her, gently squeezing her hand. "I'll lead you through the steps, and we can dance at our own pace. It's all about enjoying the moment and being in each other's company."

With a shy smile, Annalise finally nodded and said, "Okay, let's give it a try. As long as you promise not to let me embarrass myself."

"I would never let that happen," I said with a playful wink.

As I brought Annalise onto the dance floor, I guided her through the graceful steps of the waltz. Our bodies moved in sync to the music, and all worries faded away, leaving only the thrill of the moment and the warmth of our connection. Our hearts beat in rhythm with each turn around the dance floor. Embarrassment was a distant memory in our own magical world, where the only thing that mattered was the joy we found in each other's arms. My heart pounded with anticipation as I leaned in to kiss her.

Her eyes widened, and she pressed her hands over her chest as if to shield herself. Disbelief flickered across her face as her breath came in short, shallow gasps. "Clay, no," she stammered as she stepped backward.

Her words rang in the air, shattering our fragile bubble of intimacy. Rejection crushed my immortal heart as my world crumbled around me. My insides clenched in pain and confusion. I stood there, unable to move or speak. I wanted to run away, but I couldn't. My lips finally uttered, "I am sorry. I thought—forgive me." I backed away, unable to cope with the sudden shift in our relationship. With my heart shattered and my soul in shambles, I hurried toward the exit.

In a flash, Alan appeared from nowhere and grasped my arm. "Clay, what happened?" His voice laced with concern. I could see the worry in his eyes as he tightened his grip. He must have witnessed her rejection.

Internally, I struggled to find the words to explain what had happened with Annalise. Instead, I blurted out, "I can't help you anymore, Alan."

Alan took a deep breath, his voice tense. "Clay, I knew from the moment I met you both that you were meant to be together. I've watched you two from the sidelines. I've seen the way you look at her and the way she lights up when you're together. It's undeniable, and that's why I've held on for so long to finally see you two together."

I gently removed his hand from my arm and shook my head. "She just made it clear that's not what she wants." My words pierced my heart deeply. Devastation enveloped me, leaving me gasping for air. The realization that I had been holding onto an unreturned love dealt a devastating blow to my soul. "I can't be here. I have to go."

"Clay, wait. Talk to her. This must be some kind of misunderstanding. I'm sure of it."

"I am sorry, Alan." I ran away with immortal speed, fleeing the suffocating pain tearing my soul apart. Wind whipped through my hair, matching the chaos in my mind as I vanished into the night. I desperately tried to outrun the crippling anguish threatening to consume me.

The streets blurred together, reflecting my tangled emotions. I needed to find solace in the darkness. No matter how fast I ran, I couldn't escape the haunting echoes of Annalise's words, which confirmed she did not love me.

Chapter 7

Late that night, wandering the streets of downtown Los Angeles, I found myself walking into a hotel. Floor-to-ceiling windows surrounded the hotel lobby, offering a view of the city skyline, while sleek hardwood floors guided me to the reception desk. Seeing guests enter and leave the lobby, I felt alone in the world. I clutched the money clip in my pocket, wondering how far it would take me. My bank card was in the dresser drawer at home. I shuddered at the word. Was *it* still my home? The sage-green eyes of Annalise flashed through my mind, and my heart refused to beat for a few seconds.

A smile spread across the face of the woman at the front desk as she asked, "How can I help you?"

With $500 in my pocket, I asked, "What is the rate for a room for the night?"

"We offer Deluxe King rooms for $109.00 per night, which includes Wi-Fi, high-definition TV, Bluetooth, and Argan bathroom toiletries. They also have a skyline view."

"I'll book two nights," I said, sliding the cash across the counter.

She handed me a key card. "Your room is on the 7th floor, and the elevator is right across from the front desk. Checkout is Sunday at 12:00. In case you need anything while here, we have a gift shop, a boutique, and a rooftop restaurant and bar. We offer room service as well. I hope you have a wonderful stay."

After saying, "Thank you," I hurried to the elevator. I needed to be alone and surrounded by darkness and silence in order to heal.

The elevator reached the 7th floor in seconds. After finding my room, I closed the door and shut out the outside world. The room was sparsely furnished and decorated in muted colors, but none of that mattered. What mattered was the heavy weight of loneliness that suffocated me. In the silence of the room, my heart ached more and more as I thought about Annalise leaving me alone in the world. As much as I wanted her warmth and laughter, all I had now was her rejection that haunted me.

After taking off my jacket and bow tie, Annalise's face flashed in my head, and despair ravaged me. The tears streamed down my cheeks and my lips quivered as my sorrow flowed uncontrollably, blurring my vision and leaving me gasping for breath. My body convulsed as I sobbed, grief shaking me. The empty room echoing with my grief amplified my loneliness.

Curling up on the bed and hugging myself, I bawled hysterically for hours. My torment found refuge in the room, its walls bearing witness to my despair. As I lay there, I prayed for my suffering to end. The silence of the room seemed to grow louder, amplifying the emptiness surrounding me. My tears that once flowed freely were now dry trails on my cheeks. My arms tightly encircled the pillow, and I buried my face in its softness, hoping that numbness would set in.

I surrendered to my grief in the solitude, and a hollow ache echoed through every cell of my being. How could I go on without her? God gave her to me. Why had He taken her away? Had I done something wrong? I was completely and utterly alone, unable to turn to anyone.

As Death, I had never experienced sorrow or grief. I'd seen it many times through the eyes of loved ones left behind, but never through mine. What caused me to feel so overwhelmed? A heavy weight pressed down on my chest; it was a sensation unlike any I had known. Annalise's presence seemed to intertwine with my own, creating a void I couldn't comprehend. This unraveled my very being, leaving my once unyielding resolve fragile.

****

My eyes fluttered open. The heavy curtains blocked out the sunlight, giving the room a somber gloom that matched my mood. My heartbreak from last night flooded my mind, making it impossible to ignore the raw emotions that consumed me. My own despair engulfed me. Nothing could relieve my anguish. I craved drugs or alcohol to numb the pain, but my body refused to move. As I stared at the ceiling, my mind was vacant, reflecting the emptiness in my heart. I longed for Annalise. I missed her terribly. I felt nothing but loneliness, a feeling I had never encountered or imagined. I wanted someone to hear my cries and to understand my pain. I wanted to feel loved, not alone. I did not know how to cope with the pain I was experiencing. Outside, the distant sounds of traffic broke the silence, a stark contrast to the chaos inside me. The memory of Annalise's laughter lingered, deepening my torment.

I reached for my phone and then realized it was still on my dresser at home. My hands trembled. The outside world had completely disconnected from me. There were no messages, no distractions, just me and my broken heart. With each passing second, the ache in my chest intensified. I longed for the comfort of Annalise's voice and the warmth of her touch. Amidst the stillness in the room, I found myself trapped in hopelessness. I had to get out.

I forced myself to sit up and stumble toward the bathroom. As I splashed cold water on my face, I noticed my red and puffy eyes. The tailored tuxedo was a painful reminder of the night with Annalise by my side. I had hoped for a night of celebration but instead found myself in heartbreak. The suit was a reminder of her. I needed a change of clothes. The front desk clerk mentioned a boutique in the lobby. I made it my destination.

As I rounded a corner in the lobby, I discovered a small but elegant boutique. Among the racks of trendy clothing, I selected two T-shirts, two joggers, a pack of underwear, and a pair of loafers. I deliberately avoided anything that reminded me of formal attire.

Having paid for my items, I had $112 left. If needed, I could stay a third night, but I wouldn't have enough money for food or drinks. I'd have to choose between the hotel and hunger. Even more daunting than hunger was the prospect of returning home. Although I would give anything to gaze into Annalise's eyes again, the agony of reliving the rejection was unbearable. Therefore, the hotel triumphed over the food.

I returned to my hotel room and folded the cotton T-shirts and joggers and neatly arranged the clean underwear in the dresser drawers. I placed my money clip and my house keys on top of the dresser. To mask any lingering traces of her presence, I stripped out of my tuxedo and took a long, hot shower. As I changed into joggers and a T-shirt, I took a deep breath, trying to clear my head. Though I knew it was time to move on, I couldn't let her go.

As I stared at my tux, memories of the gala flooded back. The scent of her perfume lingered on my tux, bringing back memories of her dancing in my arms. Gritting my teeth, I opened my hotel door and scanned the hallway for a trash bin. I hurried over and stuffed my tuxedo into the housekeeping cart a few doors down.

The feeling that I was leaving more than my tuxedo behind haunted me as I returned to my room. A mixture of relief and sadness washed over me as I sank into the chair. I struggled to forget her but wondered if I could ever truly do so. I needed a drink, something to numb the pain and make me forget, if only for a short time.

The elevator took me to the top floor, leading directly into the outdoor rooftop bar and restaurant. As the sun set in the background, string lighting created a soft glow on the pergola eaves. Palm trees and cacti surrounded the intimate booths and tables. The glass railing enclosing the restaurant and bar offered views of the skyline. My vantage point offered a glimpse of the towering skyscrapers and shimmering lights far in the distance. The lights mesmerized me, making everything else seem to fade into the background.

A hostess with blonde hair and red lips ushered me to a small table by the railing. "Mick will be your server. Enjoy your meal," she said, handing me a menu.

Although the view was picturesque, my thoughts drifted back to my woes. I planned to drench my sorrows in whiskey.

"Hi, my name is Mick. I'll be your server. Are you ready to order?"

"Yes, I'll have a whiskey, straight up."

"May I suggest our cheeseburger sliders and fries to go with your whiskey?" he asked.

Mick's suggestion caught my attention, and I nodded. "That would be great. Thank you."

"I'll be back with your whiskey."

A few minutes later, Mick returned and placed the glass in front of me. A faint caramel scent wafted upward, tempting me further. As he hurried away, I took a sip. The smooth whiskey slid down my throat, leaving a trail of warmth that calmed my racing thoughts. Looking at the glass, I wondered how many more I would need to heal my pain.

When Mick delivered my food, I placed another order for whiskey. As I pushed my food around my plate, I gazed out at the twinkling city lights. A temporary respite emerged from the whiskey. The amber liquid was healing and haunting, bringing a bittersweet mix of solace and longing with every sip. I closed my eyes to try to make sense of my feelings. My only option was to accept the reality of the situation. But could I do so? Every part of my soul knew I couldn't.

"Aren't you being a bit dramatic?"

I knew that voice. As my eyelids flew open, I looked up at Domiel sitting across from me. His chestnut hair perfectly framed his striking green eyes, and the dim lighting illuminated his beard. Despite the whiskey numbing my senses, I resented him for intruding on my privacy.

He raised an eyebrow and leaned back in his chair, studying me with amusement. Sarcasm laced his voice, piercing my self-pity bubble. "You know, drowning your sorrows in whiskey won't change your situation."

"Domiel, what are you doing here?"

Before he could respond, Mick approached and asked, "I see you have a guest with you. May I take your order?"

"I'll have a Manhattan, please. Nothing to eat. Thank you."

"Of course, I'll be right back with your drink."

Domiel turned his attention back to me. His gaze locked on mine as if he could see right through me, unraveling all of my torment and grief. "It's true that I came to speak with you about my dilemma, but you're obviously troubled. We will tackle your concerns first." Domiel glanced at my attire, his eyebrows twitching in surprise. It was clear he expected to find me in my expensive clothes, not casual attire. "What happened to the Armani suit?"

I waved his question away. "It doesn't matter. What dilemma?"

He shook his head. "No, you first. Why so glum?"

Annalise flashed in my mind's eye, replaying the exact moment she rejected my advances. I shuddered as I tried to push the memory away, but it relentlessly refused to let go. The wretched feeling consumed me like a gaping hole that couldn't be filled. "I can't talk about it," I murmured.

Mick returned and put Domiel's drink on the table. Domiel nodded in acknowledgment before taking a sip and sighing. "I love Manhattans." He looked at me and said, "You know you can talk to me about anything."

"It's too painful," I whispered, my voice barely audible over the soft hum of conversation around us.

"I understand that pain can be overwhelming but sometimes sharing it with someone can help lighten the load. I am here to support you no matter what," Domiel said with genuine concern.

"I have feelings for someone, but they aren't reciprocated," I blurted out.

"You're mistaken."

"What do you mean?"

"I mean, you're wrong," Domiel said in a confident tone, his gaze unwavering. "I've seen how she looks at you when she thinks no one is watching. Trust me, there's more to this than meets the eye."

"What? How do you know that?" I asked, furrowing my brows.

"Have you forgotten that I watch over you, little brother?"

As if I hadn't heard him right, I cocked my head. My mind raced, trying to comprehend Domiel's words. Why had he called me his brother? We had no familial ties. The confusion must have been evident on my face, as Domiel's eyes softened as he said, "You truly don't remember?"

"No."

"We are brothers. Our family is large, and you were always Father's favorite."

"I have a father?"

"God is our Father, and we are His angels. Father and Mother gave us life, and despite our superiority over mankind, they raised us to protect them. You were always curious about the purpose of human existence. Why this? Why that? The questions never stopped. Father sent you down to Earth on your twenty-third birthday to guide departed human souls into the afterlife."

A wave of dizziness hit me, and I slumped in my chair, my mind a jumbled mess of puzzle pieces refusing to fit together. A sea of uncertainty clouded my brain as I tried to grasp what was going on. It seemed impossible to comprehend the revelation of a divine father and the idea of being an angel.

Domiel scooted his chair closer to mine and gently rested his hand on my quaking shoulders. "Our Father guides us, and our purpose on Earth is to fulfill his mission."

"Why am I unable to recall something so significant?" I uttered.

"The years on Earth seemed to have affected your perception. I suppose it's time I awakened your memories."

A spark of light erupted from his index finger as he pointed it at my forehead, warming my skin. *Mountains of greenery, waterfalls, and castles flooded into my mind. I was running through a castle as Domiel chased me. Warm sunlight streamed through the stained-glass windows, casting vibrant colors on the floor. The sound of our footsteps echoing on the marble floors and our laughter bouncing off the walls infused the air with mischief. In that moment, I realized that Domiel was not just a friend but a long-lost brother from a forgotten realm.*

Our path led us into a dining room filled with my siblings seated at a long table. There was something distinctive about each sibling, from Dahlia's fiery red cascading curls to Domiel's striking green eyes. A golden chandelier cast a warm glow over the family gathering, while fine china and crystal glasses reflected the flickering candlelight on the table.

We ran around the room, and our Father's tall frame loomed over us, casting a long shadow across the floor. His broad shoulders and commanding presence made Him seem even taller as He wrapped His arms around us. He gently ushered us into our seats as He took his seat at the head of the table. His curly, golden-brown hair caught the overhead light as His olive-green eyes smiled at each of us. Mother sat at the opposite end. I bore an uncanny resemblance to her with my pale blue eyes and dark brown hair.

Together, their ethereal radiance illuminated the room, casting a soft light that embraced us all. As Father prayed, we gathered our hands to remember that acceptance and respect for our differences were at the core of our existence.

Father looked back and forth between us as He said, "A wise man once said that true beauty lies in celebrating our differences." He paused for a moment before continuing. "That's what makes the world beautiful and harmonious."

"Remember, my children, that our realm has always been intertwined with the human world," Mother said gently. "It is our duty to guide and protect them, for they are the key to maintaining the balance between our realms."

As her words settled in my heart, I felt a sense of purpose and a newfound understanding of my place in the world.

In the midst of taking a bite of food, Father asked, "What shall we discuss?"

"Humans!" I shouted in delight.

Dahlia flipped her fiery red locks over her shoulder. They cascaded down her back like flames, drawing attention to her vibrant turquoise eyes, reflecting her lively spirit. "That's what you always say," she retorted with a smirk.

Hugging myself, I said, "I love humans. They fascinate me."

Domiel huffed. "You play with them as if they were dolls."

"I don't play with them," I corrected. "I watch over them."

He waved me away.

My memories faded, and I found myself back in the present, staring at Domiel. "I'm an angel," I murmured.

"Yes, and your name is Azrael, not Death, as you call yourself, or Clay, as your lovely human angel calls you." Domiel sighed, his eyes filled with sadness. "Your task on Earth is not an effortless one, Azrael. You witness pain, suffering, heartbreak, and loss. You carry the burden of guiding souls to their final destination, offering them solace and peace in their last moments. It's a sacred duty, one that requires immense compassion and strength. This may also be the reason you've repressed your past."

"Possibly." His comment about Annalise resurfaced in my mind: *There's more to this situation than meets the eye.* What had he meant? As I pondered Domiel's words, a deep sense of curiosity washed over me. Did he know something I did not? What had he meant?

Domiel's eyes flickered with understanding as he stared at me. "You're wondering what I know about her. Well, I know that she did not reject you."

"If you were observing us, you would have noticed her horrified expression as she retreated from me while I attempted to kiss her." The words I uttered pierced me like a blade. The pain intensified as I remembered her body recoiling from my touch.

"Yes, I was watching. You gave her the wrong impression."

"How could she misinterpret a kiss?"

"Do you not recall how you sent her on her way?"

"That's different."

"Is it?" Domiel gently said. "The only kiss she has ever experienced was when you released her human soul into the afterlife. What you witnessed was not rejection but shock and confusion."

My eyes widened as a chill ran down my spine. Had Annalise thought my kiss meant to send her away again? Remorse and humiliation swept over me as I realized what I had done. Unknowingly, I had triggered her deepest fears, leading her to believe that my touch had meant the end of her life. How was I so blind to my actions' consequences? I fled like a coward. She never had a chance to explain. I just left her. Internally, I vowed to mend the damage I caused. I looked at Domiel. "I must go to her."

"Brother, you don't have to look far. She desperately awaits your return at the home you both share."

Chapter 8

I led Domiel into our living room. At this point in the day, the sun's rays streamed through the floor-to-ceiling windows, highlighting the wood patterns of the coffee table and all the lush indoor plants Annalise placed around the room, not to mention the plush, oversized earth-tone sofas covered with throw pillows.

As the silence of the house surrounded me, I panicked, fearing Annalise had abandoned me. Then the sound of footsteps rushing down the hall sent my heart racing. As I turned, I laid my eyes on Annalise running toward me. I stared into her red, puffy eyes, speechless.

"You left me on my birthday!" she shouted.

"No, I thought," I stammered, "you didn't want me."

Tears welled up in her eyes, and her voice quivered as she cried, "No, it was *you* who didn't want *me*!"

The suffocating weight of guilt settled in my chest as I witnessed the pain I had caused her. My internal vow was to never hurt her. "That's not true. I tried to kiss you, but you rejected me."

A contorted look crossed her face, somewhere between anger, hurt, or betrayal. "You were sending me back!"

My voice rose as I desperately tried to convey my true intentions. "No. I wanted to feel the warmth of your lips against mine and express the depth of my affection through a passionate and lingering kiss."

She shed more tears before blinking them away. "What?"

"I love you, Annalise."

"I love you too," she whispered, her voice full of vulnerability.

As if holding its breath, the room fell silent. Annalise reached out slowly, her trembling hand touching mine. A shiver ran down my spine as I traced the outline of her lips. She moaned sweetly and sank into my arms. Our tongues danced in a heated embrace as our lips slammed together. She tasted intoxicating, a delicious blend of sweetness and desire. Passion burned inside me, replacing pain with pleasure. The universe maintained perfect balance once again during that lovesick moment.

Domiel shattered our intimacy. His deep, booming voice filled the room as he demanded our attention. "All right, lovebirds. We still need to solve my dilemma."

Annalise's face paled when she realized someone else was in the room. "What's going on? Who is he?" she whispered into my ear.

With a mischievous grin on his face, Domiel extended his hand. "I am Domiel, the brother of Azrael—whom you have named Clay."

"I do not understand," she said, shifting her gaze between Domiel and me.

"We're angels, my dear. Azrael is the Angel of Death, and I am Father's messenger," Domiel explained, his eyes shimmering with otherworldly light.

"Your father is…God?" she stammered in disbelief, her grip tightening around my arm.

"Yes, and as you recall, Father transformed you into an angel and sent you back to Earth as a gift for Azrael."

Annalise stared at me in awe and confusion as I remained silent. "But you told me that you couldn't recall your birth or the process of becoming Death."

Before I could respond, Domiel answered, "Azrael had no memory of his past. I had to clear the blockage from his mind and restore his memories. Therefore, he told you what he believed to be true."

She brushed her hand along my cheek. "I love you even more."

As I lowered my head to kiss her, Domiel stepped between us. "Enough kissing. As I stated, I came here to discuss my dilemma with you, Azrael. Now that we have resolved yours, can we discuss mine?"

"Yes, of course," I replied, reluctantly tearing my gaze away from Annalise. "What's your dilemma, Domiel?"

His eyes narrowed, and his voice deepened as he said, "Father watched over you, Azrael, with Annalise. He has decided that angels should live among humans and interact with them."

In unison, Annalise and I said, "What's wrong with that?" We glanced at each other and exchanged high fives.

He smirked. "I see now. You two are perfect for each other." He paused before continuing. "Let me return to my situation and explain. We consider ourselves a higher species. God did not intend for us to coexist with humans. Living on Earth will erode our status and dilute our minds, as it did yours, Azrael. The angels do not want this. Some are rebellious and have threatened retaliation and war."

Shaking my head, I asked, "Why a war?"

He stated with a stern stare, "We believe that integrating with humans will compromise our divine purpose. This may lead to an eventual conflict between angels and humans. Angels will destroy mankind and win."

"How do I fit into this impending conflict between angels and humans?"

"You're going to stop this."

"Me? How?"

"You're like Father. Humans fascinate you, and you understand both angelic and human perspectives. You are the golden boy. That is why He let you descend to Earth and gave you Annalise." Domiel's eyes brimmed with hope as he leaned in closer. "You can bridge the gap. You must convince Him that coexistence is impossible."

"Domiel, I've lived on Earth for centuries. How can I convince Father when I have embraced humanity and forgotten my own divine nature?"

"It was your choice to live among humans. We do not share that desire. Angels will fight against this, and humans will become targets. You must ensure Father understands that this will put His precious humans in danger."

"Does resisting His wishes not pose the same danger?"

"Will you at least speak with Him?" Domiel pleaded, running his hands over his beard.

I sighed, accepting the burden. "I'll do my best to convince Him."

He took my hands in his as he said, "Thank you."

****

After Domiel left, I exhaled deeply.

"Are you really going to speak to God?" Annalise pursed her lips as she drew her brows together.

"You look worried."

"Well, I mean. Would you have to go to Heaven?"

I placed my hand on her shoulder and gently squeezed it. "I planned to speak to Him at church."

"Right, I should have thought of that. I just assumed…" She sighed.

My arms wrapped around her. "I'm never leaving you again. Ever."

"Promise me," she said, looking up at me with those sage-green eyes.

"You have my word."

She hugged me tightly. "I've always wanted this—to be with you."

I held her close and said, "I've always wanted this too."

She yawned, breaking away and saying, "I haven't slept very well since you left."

"Same here. I think I need a nap."

She laughed. "Me too."

We climbed the stairs together to our bedroom. Her lips caught my attention as I gazed at them. A tingling sensation spread through my entire body when my lips touched hers. She drew me close and ran her fingers through my hair as I moaned with pleasure.

I looked into her eyes and whispered, "We can take things slow."

She stepped away from me and took off her T-shirt. "This is my first time, and with the man I love. What if I don't want to take things slow?"

I stripped naked in seconds. Her clothes came off just as quickly. I picked her up and gently laid her on the bed beneath me. I kissed her lips, neck, and breasts, savoring the scent of her skin. My lips trailed down her stomach, giving her goosebumps, until I reached her inner thighs. She arched her back and drew me closer, whispering, "Clay, you're driving me crazy."

In between kisses, I said, "I'm trying to."

"But I want you—to feel you. Make love to me."

"As you wish."

The moment I entered her, I surrendered my heart and soul. I gazed into her eyes and caressed every inch of her body. Passion and desire ignited a burning heat between us. As the world faded away, we clung to each other, lost in pure ecstasy.

The warmth of her body against mine created a comforting cocoon as we lay entangled in each other's arms. Her sweet scent lingered on my skin, a reminder of the love we just shared. The soft rhythm of her breathing matched the gentle rise and fall of her chest, lulling me into a deep, peaceful sleep.

The last remnants of the sunset warmed the room as I opened my eyes. A deep breath escaped my mouth as I savored the moment. The sensation of waking up with Annalise in my arms overwhelmed me completely. Her hair falling against her peaceful expression as she slept quickened my heart. While tracing my fingers along the contours of her beautiful face, I roused her from sleep.

Laughing softly, she brushed my hair off my forehead. "I like your tousled hair."

"You're so beautiful. Are you happy?" I asked, tucking a loose strand of her hair behind her ear.

"Very happy," she said, snuggling closer.

"You complete me."

"I love you, Clay. Oops. Should I call you Azrael?"

No matter what name she called me, I would answer. "I love it when you call me Clay." As I placed my hand over my heart, I confessed, "I am completely, deeply, and utterly in love with you." I seemed to have accessed a secret place in her heart for only me as her eyes shimmered with unshed tears. "Can I ask you something?"

"Anything."

"Will you come with me to church tonight? I haven't spoken to my Father in a long time, and I'm a bit nervous."

"We'll face this together, Clay," she said gently, squeezing my hand. "I'll be by your side, every step of the way."

Chapter 9

As we walked out the front door, I clicked the remote to unlock the Hummer. I offered Annalise my hand as she stepped onto the runner. Her long, brown hair cascaded down her shoulders, contrasting beautifully with her taupe cargo pants and black shirt. A smile played on her lips as she settled into the plush seating. My heart raced with affection as I softly kissed her. As the engine rumbled in time with my heartbeat, I pulled away from the curb.

"Which church are we going to?"

"Cathedral of Promise. My first encounter with Father Logan was while I was releasing a soul into the afterlife. As a result, he saw me for who I really am. I am now his go-to person whenever he has a soul in need."

She twisted her body in surprise, staring at me. "You told a priest that you are Death?"

I shrugged. "Is that so odd?"

After a moment of silence, she said, "I guess not."

"He took it rather well," I laughed.

"Is he aware that you're stopping by tonight? Is the church unlocked or is there an evening mass?"

"There's no mass scheduled. The church will be locked, and no, I didn't inform him. As you know, my gift allows me to temporarily eliminate pain, pause the passing of souls, and finally guide them into the afterlife. However, I can also alter objects with my thoughts, so a lock will not be a problem," I explained to Annalise.

"Do all angels possess special powers?"

"My siblings do. Dahlia can brighten or dim light and create illusions with her gaze. Domiel can control the elements, manipulating fire, water, and air at will. With a single touch, Leilani can mend broken bones and cure illnesses. Jahoel's mind can accelerate or pause time, freezing the world around him. Orifiel has the unique ability to erase, restore, and alter memories in humans' minds. Zaphkiel can become invisible at will, enabling him to move undetected by humans and angels alike."

She listened intently to my every word with open eyes and parted lips as she processed the extraordinary powers of my siblings and me.

"Each of us possesses superhuman strength, senses, and speed, but the most intriguing aspect of our immortality is that, after reaching 21 years old, we never age. We seem to defy the passage of time."

"Do *I* possess superpowers?"

Turning to look at her, I said softly, "You have power over my heart."

Her eyes welled up with tears as her hand trembled over her own heart. "That's the most beautiful thing anyone has ever said to me. I will cherish your heart and protect it forever."

I too struggled to hold back tears as her words touched the deepest parts of my soul. I mimicked her words. "And that is also the most beautiful thing anyone has ever said to me." Taking her hand, I gazed at her before returning my attention to the road. Silence reigned throughout the remainder of the drive.

The Cathedral of Promise towered into the night sky, casting a shadow on the street below. The streetlights illuminated the ivy climbing up the stone facade and over the grand wooden doors.

Trees lined the pathways leading to the entrance, their branches swaying in the evening breeze.

After pulling up to the curb and turning off the engine, I unlocked Annalise's door. Stepping onto the sidewalk, she gazed at the cathedral with wide eyes. As we approached the majestic wooden doors, the soft glow of the stained-glass windows danced across her skin. Concentrating my thoughts on the door, I invoked my telekinetic abilities. A tingling sensation ran through my fingertips as I manipulated the latch. With a snap of the metal, the hinges creaked, and the heavy wooden door slowly opened. A disbelieving smile spread across Annalise's face as I led her through the door and into the empty church.

Under the vaulted ceiling adorned with biblical paintings, we approached the altar. Moonlight filtered through the stained glass, highlighting the natural stone floors in a kaleidoscope of colors. The fragrance of incense and the reflections of candle sconces on the aged walls added to the tranquil setting as we sat in one of the pews.

Closing my eyes, I gathered my thoughts to make Domiel's case to our Father. His and our siblings' refusal to do as Father asked would be difficult to convey. Both angels and humans depended on my ability to communicate this conflict's urgency and potential devastation. As each moment elapsed, the weight of my responsibilities intensified, as if the resolution was entirely dependent on me.

"Are you praying or talking to God?" Annalise inquired, interrupting my thoughts. Both frustration and affection welled up within me, and I opened my eyes and stared at her. Her ability to effortlessly disrupt my deepest thoughts captivated me, a testament to her power over me. "Neither," I replied. "I'm gathering my thoughts on how to plead Domiel's case. Your interruption reminded me of how much I value you being alongside me during this uncertain time."

She snuggled closer to me and squeezed my hand.

Once again, I closed my eyes, my thoughts drifting to the matter at hand. Father's wrath demanded a delicate approach from me. As I breathed deeply, I began to focus, considering every word carefully.

"Are you talking to Him right now?"

In exasperation, I replied, "Not yet, my love, but if you keep interrupting me, I may never find the right words to influence Father's judgment."

"Well, maybe I can help you find the right words," she whispered playfully, her warm breath tickling my ear.

Despite my frustration, I smiled at her persistence. "Would you prefer I speak my thoughts aloud, Annalise?"

She nodded curtly, "Yes."

"Very well. My first thought was to apologize for neglecting my family due to my intense involvement with humans. I have begun to realize that the earthly realm had cast a spell over me, clouding my memory, and I had forgotten the cherished bond I once shared with my divine family."

"I wouldn't say that. You don't know why your memory was erased. Perhaps God discovered that your interaction with humanity could lead to growth and empathy. Therefore, He temporarily severed your ties to the heavenly realm."

As I stared blankly at her, I couldn't comprehend her words. How could Father be so willing to separate me from my family? Was it punishment for my curiosity about humans? I struggled to find meaning in her revelation, but it only deepened the ache in my heart. "I can't believe my Father would do this," I exclaimed.

"I didn't mean it to be cruel," she replied gently. "I just think God doesn't need an apology," she added. "I would directly address Domiel's and the other angels' threats of war," she said. "Say they consider humanity a threat to their kingdom and are willing to do whatever it takes to eliminate it."

"We must handle this delicate situation with care and tact," I responded, my mind buzzing with ideas. "Instead of focusing on the threat, we should emphasize the potential for reconciliation and understanding between humans and celestial beings that leads to a peaceful resolution."

"There's nothing peaceful about this whole mess. It doesn't look like Domiel will give in. It's either his way or war."

I knew the key to convincing my Father was to appeal to his compassion for humans. "Forcing angels to live on Earth wasn't the most effective way to create a bond between them. Perhaps we could create a council of celestial beings and humans that would address conflicts and find common ground. In this manner, we could prevent potential destruction, death, and suffering."

She sighed. "There you go again."

"Sorry. My mind is racing. We can't put Him on the defensive. Starting off with war isn't wise."

"Sugarcoating won't solve it either."

"Hello, my son, Annalise."

Our heads jerked toward the divine voice. Father stood at the altar. A shimmer of soft light surrounded Him, confirming His presence. His olive-green eyes shone with wisdom, while the lines etched on His face revealed both joy and sorrow. Some strands of His golden-brown hair curled rebelliously, while others lay smoothly, creating a harmonious chaos that reflected His complex nature. A cozy gray sweater and dark pants added a touch of humanity to His otherwise serene appearance.

My mind recalled memories of His love and understanding for mankind as I saw His expression.

He glided effortlessly across the natural stone flooring as He approached. I rose to greet Him, and as I wrapped my arms around Him, peace washed over me. The burden lifted from my shoulders, replaced by a profound sense of love and acceptance. While cradled in my Father's arms—earthly and divine—I knew He knew all about Domiel's rebellion.

When my Father turned to embrace Annalise, her eyes sparkled with joy. In that moment, I couldn't help but marvel at how my Father had transformed our lives.

His voice echoed with authority, "Well, you've got my attention. I'm eager to hear Domiel's perspective and understand his rebellion. Why has he not addressed his concerns directly to me? It is imperative for my children to communicate their thoughts and emotions with me."

As Father finished speaking, Leilani, Orifiel, and Zaphkiel entered the church with Domiel. An energy shift fell over the church as my siblings paraded down the aisle, dragging human slaves mercilessly. Five women, three men, and two children, all clinging to leashes, followed them. As the humans' eyes darted around, their bodies shook with uncontrollable fear. A man hovered protectively over a boy and a girl. The boy clutched the girl's hand tightly, his golden hair tousled, his blue eyes wide with fear. Golden curls framed her pale, freckled face as her blue eyes blinked rapidly. Both sobbed as they clung to the man. The adults fared no better, with their mouths agape, clenched teeth, and sweat dripping down their foreheads.

When the submissive, docile humans followed my siblings without hesitation, my heart pounded with horror and shock. The path Domiel was on was dark and twisted. How could he and my siblings commit such an inhumane and degrading act? What must I do? I must stop them. I must save these helpless beings.

A blaze of rage spread across Father's face as He stared at Domiel with bulging eyes. The air crackled around Him as He yelled loudly, "Domiel, how dare you bring these innocent people here against their will?"

As Domiel marched forward, towing along a human, he boasted, "It's time to see what Father's plan looks like."

Domiel had betrayed me. I trembled as I watched my own brother reveal his true colors and stand defiantly before our Father. The smugness in his eyes and the sight of the bruised and trembling human at his side intensified my anger. "You used me to get to Father."

Domiel shook his head dismissively. "That's right, little brother," he said. "I did what I had to do."

I hissed, my gaze fixed on Domiel. "This is madness. Our purpose is to safeguard humanity, not to take advantage of it. It's not too late to redeem yourself. Don't continue on this dark path."

In the midst of my sentence, my siblings Dahlia and Jahoel ran into the church and joined Father's side. Loyalty and determination shone in their eyes. The tension in the room intensified as their presence reflected the divide within our celestial family.

Dahlia's eyes radiated power, and her voice echoed with authority. "Domiel, you have strayed from our purpose and forsaken the very essence of our existence. We cannot stand by while you unleash chaos on humanity. We will fight to protect them, even if it means turning against our own kind. I implore you to let them go."

In contrast to his short, raven-black hair and benevolent gray eyes, Jahoel's chiseled features and fierce gaze commanded supremacy and respect. The sound of his firm, unwavering voice filled the room. "Domiel, our purpose was to serve as protectors, not oppressors. Release these people."

Domiel's wicked grin widened. "Oh, my dear siblings, you fail to understand. This is just the beginning. I am determined to show Father the consequences of His plan, no matter what the cost." His voice dripped with venom as he continued, "I will unleash chaos upon this human world, and there will be no escape."

A glowing silhouette appeared beside Father, solidifying into a woman. As I blinked, my mother appeared. Her pale blue orbs shone with intensity and locked onto Domiel. With sadness and disappointment in her voice, she spoke softly. "My son, what has happened to you? Darkness and malice have now replaced the love and compassion that once flowed through your celestial veins. You are choosing a path that will only destroy you, not bring you redemption. Please reconsider your actions and remember who you once were."

Domiel's expression softened as he gazed at our mother, but his anger quickly returned. A bitter laugh escaped his lips as he shook his head, saying, "You've always been blind when it comes to Father, Mother. I will continue to expose the flaws in His plan until He backs off, even if it means defying our celestial family."

As Father whispered something into Mother's ear, divine light enveloped her, and within moments, she vanished, leaving only a faint sparkle behind.

Annalise connected her fingers with mine. It wasn't until that moment that I realized she was standing next to me. She trembled slightly, and fear reflected in her saucer-widened eyes as she whispered, "I'm scared, Clay."

I gently squeezed her hand, offering reassurance. Before I could speak, a blast of celestial light engulfed the church, illuminating every corner. The air crackled with unearthly energy, shattering stained glass and spraying glittering fragments everywhere. Echoes of the explosion rattled the church's foundation as moonlight streamed through the broken windows.

The leashes snapped like brittle twigs from the powerful impact, instantly releasing the humans. Taking flight from the church, they scrambled to safety, screaming. The man with the two kids collapsed, clutching his chest. In tears, the boy and girl huddled near him. A jagged glass shard glistened under the moonlight as it protruded from his chest. Blood smeared his clothes and stained the natural stone flooring as it pooled around him. I hurried toward him, with Annalise trailing closely behind. Using all his remaining strength, he gripped my hand with trembling fingers. Blood filled his mouth, and his voice was barely a whisper. He pleaded with his last breath, "Save my children."

"Run! Get them outside!" I yelled after scooping up his children and throwing them into Annalise's arms.

Grabbing my arm, she cried, "Not without you."

"I'll be fine. Go!"

She stared at me for several seconds, her gaze begging, as if deciding whether to stay or go. Annalise's footsteps were slow and deliberate as she led the kids away, surrendering to my wishes. The girl cried out, "Dad!" The boy clutched his sister's hand, trying to be brave, but his tear-stained face showed his anguish. Annalise continued to walk toward the exit, leading the children further away from their father. She glanced back over her shoulder before passing through the door.

As I kneeled down beside the fallen man and released his soul into the afterlife, a sense of sorrow filled me. The weight of grief settled on my shoulders as I stood up, my eyes narrowing with determination. I swore to avenge his death.

A second burst of light ignited the church, sending me flying backward, crashing into the pews with a bone-jarring thud and gasping for air. The world spun in a dizzy blur around me as I lay there unable to catch my breath. Dazed, I couldn't make sense of what had just happened.

Jahoel offered me his hand and asked, "Are you alright?"

"What are these blasts of light? Are they weapons or divine intervention?" My panic intensified as I shook off my bewilderment and demanded, "And why are they targeting us specifically?"

Jahoel clarified, saying, "Domiel and Father are responsible, and we are caught in the crossfire."

Dahlia hurried toward us; her eyes fierce with determination as another burst of light rocked the church. The stone walls groaned under pressure, sending tremors through the foundation. "This recklessness has the potential to destroy the fundamental structure of the universe," she cautioned. "Domiel needs to stop trying to prove Father wrong before he causes irreversible damage."

I turned in a circle, viewing the church. We were the only ones left. The shattered stained-glass windows cast an eerie pattern of light across the floor. Chunks of wood from broken pews littered the aisle. The once sacred space now looked like a war zone. "Where are Father and Domiel? Where are the others?"

Jahoel's eyes darted around the chaotic scene, and he clenched his jaw. "I believe Father retreated with Domiel and our other siblings to prevent further collateral damage."

"That means we're on our own in the middle of this madness," Dahlia pointed out.

My thoughts turned to Annalise and the two kids. "I told Annalise to get out of the church. Would the blasts affect the outside?" I didn't wait for a response as I ran to the doors.

"We'll go with you," Jahoel called after me.

Opening the heavy wooden doors revealed more chaos. The sky was a swirling vortex of dark clouds. All the streetlights were out, their shattered bulbs littering the ground like fallen stars. The church courtyard was a scene of devastation, with trees uprooted and the air thick with smoke and debris from burning buildings. As the divine onslaught raged, people ran in every direction looking for shelter. My heart pounded frantically as I scanned the crowd, shouting, "Annalise! Where are you?"

The expressions on Jahoel's and Dahlia's faces mirrored my anxiety. "Let's split up," Jahoel said. "We'll cover more ground that way."

Dahlia nodded in agreement.

Just then, I spotted Annalise in the distance. The two children clung to her; their faces streaked with tears. Their once golden locks were now dull gray, with soot clinging to each strand. Amidst the turmoil, their innocent faces appeared even more tragic. I sprinted toward them, dodging fallen branches and debris, screaming her name, "Annalise!"

Within seconds, she turned and ran toward me, dragging the children behind her. We collided in a desperate embrace, the children wedged between us. I kissed her forehead and asked, "Are you okay?"

"I was so worried," Annalise whispered as she nodded, tears welling up in her eyes. "Thank God you are safe!" she cried, hugging me even tighter.

As Jahoel and Dahlia scanned the area, their eyes remained focused and determined.

"We can't stay out in the open," said Jahoel as he studied the churning sky.

In her ever-vigilant manner, Dahlia pointed to a nearby parking garage. "We can take cover there until we are sure there are no more blasts. We must move quickly," she insisted.

As we hurried toward it, the ground shook with another blast, sending a fresh wave of panic through the crowd. Weaving between panicked people and fallen debris, I tightened my grip on Annalise's hand and made sure the children were secure between us. The parking garage loomed ahead, a concrete sanctuary amid the destruction. Upon reaching the entrance, Jahoel and Dahlia searched the area for any immediate threats before ushering us inside. The garage offered a momentary respite from the pandemonium outside.

Darkness shrouded the garage, making it difficult to see more than a few feet ahead. The only light came from the occasional flicker of distant fires outside, casting eerie shadows on the concrete walls. We settled down under the entrance archway. As our eyes adjusted to the darkness, we could see the silhouettes of other families huddled together, their faces etched with fear and uncertainty. Jahoel quickly gathered some old crates and arranged them into makeshift seating.

"My dad isn't coming, is he? He died, didn't he?" the boy asked. His large blue eyes were filled with dread.

His expression made my heart ache with the truth I had to convey. I kneeled down to place my hand on his shoulder. "I'm so sorry. Yes, your father has passed away."

Trying to hold back tears, the boy nodded bravely.

The girl's blue eyes mirrored the boy's, as disbelief etched across her young face. "He's dead?"

Pausing, I tried to find the right words, but only the truth filled my head. "Yes, he is," I said gently, "but he loved you both and would want you to stay strong."

Annalise joined us, wrapping her arms around the children, providing comfort.

Dahlia crouched beside them, her eyes softening for a moment as she added, "We will protect you, and together, we will find a way through this."

The echoes of another distant blast reached us, and the garage floor rumbled beneath our feet. I squeezed the children's hands, shifting their attention to me instead of the startling quakes threatening us.

Anger flashed in Jahoel's eyes. "Why is Father allowing Domiel to cause such havoc on innocent lives? He could have intervened long ago and prevented all of this suffering. What is stopping Him?"

I glared at Jahoel. The children were already in a state of panic, and I was trying to keep them calm, not arouse more fear.

"Despite not knowing what it is, we must believe that there is a greater plan at work," Dahlia offered, her approach more positive.

He exhaled slowly, the tension in his shoulders easing slightly. "Perhaps you're right, Dahlia," he conceded, though doubt still lingered in his voice. "But with so much chaos and pain around us, it's challenging to see the bigger picture."

Keeping my focus on the children, I watched their blue eyes light up with a frantic look as they surveyed the chaotic scene surrounding them.

"What are your names?" I asked gently, distracting them.

"I'm Theo, and this is my sister, Willow," said the boy.

"How old are you?" I inquired.

Theo responded hesitantly, "I'm 10, and Willow is 9."

Willow clung to his arm, her eyes watering.

"We need to get in touch with your mother. How can I get in touch with her?"

"We don't know where our mother is," Theo clarified, his voice on edge. "It's been us and Dad for a long time."

"Our parents are divorced," Willow explained, her voice barely above a whisper.

Theo clenched his jaw as he struggled to hold back tears. With bitterness flickering across his face, he added, "She left us. If she didn't want us then, she won't want us now."

Willow looked at him sorrowfully, her grip on his arm tightening. "It's okay," she said softly.

The concern in Annalise's eyes echoed the worry churning within me. Her slight, almost undetectable nod encouraged me to continue comforting the children. They had lost their father, and my heart ached for them. Without other family members, where would they go? I forced calm into my voice as I said, "Theo and Willow, we'll figure this out together. For now, you're safe with us."

It was evident that their bond was deep as they clung to each other, offering unspoken reinforcements. Their vulnerability as they held me close to them was a moment that would never fade from my memory. They'd be much better off if we could get them to a safe, secure place. If I could get to my Hummer, I could transport everyone to safety within the walls of our home. I pulled Annalise, Jahoel, and Dahlia aside and explained my plan to them. "I believe I can make it to the Hummer. I will drive back here and take everyone to our house. It will be a much safer environment for Theo and Willow."

"But what about the streets?" Annalise asked, her voice on edge. "Are they safe? And how do you know our house is safer?"

"I'll be quick and careful," I assured her. "Father and Domiel were in the church when the blasts started. I believe the focus of all the commotion is the church. Our home is farther away, and we have plenty of food and supplies for everyone, and there we can strategize our next moves."

"I'll go with you to the Hummer," Jahoel said. A firm nod reflected his resolve. "We'll be safer together," he added.

As Dahlia gazed at the children, her protective instincts kicked in. "I'll stay here. Annalise and I will closely monitor them until your return."

"So we're all in agreement?" I asked.

"I'm in," Jahoel said.

"Yes," Dahila said.

I turned to Annalise and pulled her into my arms, holding her close to my heart. Her warm skin against mine contrasted starkly with the cold dread looming over us. She shuddered, uncovering the apprehension she tried to conceal. My lips brushed against her ear as I whispered, "We'll be back before you know it."

She held me for a moment longer before she whispered back, "Please be careful."

I squeezed her hand, and said, "I promise." I turned to Jahoel. "Let's move out."

"You're leaving? Where are you going?" Theo asked.

"We're just going to get my Hummer, Theo," I explained gently. "We need it to move everyone to a safer place. Stay with Dahlia and Annalise, okay?" I ruffled his hair and said, "Protect your sister."

He nodded. "Okay, as long as you promise to come back."

"I promise." This was my second promise of the night. Breaking either promise was not an option.

Before leaving the garage, I glanced back at Annalise. Theo and Willow stood on either side of her. As I waved, Annalise's eyes teared up, while Theo wrapped his arm around Willow's shoulders. Willow smiled bravely, although she tightened her grip on Theo's hand. Dahlia stood tall, with the strength and valor of a warrior. Her vigilance fortified my resolve as I stepped into the night.

Jahoel and I made our way toward the Hummer, broken glass crunched beneath our shoes, and sirens echoed in the distance. A pungent stench of smoke and chemicals caused by the fire filled the air, serving as a reminder of the devastation that had just occurred. Firefighters cleared fallen trees and debris from the street as they extinguished flames popping up among the embers. In the pitch-black night, the faint glow of the moon and flashing lights from emergency vehicles illuminated the soot-covered buildings with their windows broken and walls scorched.

Several feet down the street, I spotted my Hummer covered in ash, yet otherwise fine. As I ran toward it and reached the door, I clicked the remote control, and we jumped inside. While I started the engine, we exchanged glances, silently conveying our concerns. It looked like a war zone, but more concerning was the effect this horrendous scene would have on people. Most probably knew nothing of angels, let alone an apocalyptic war between humans and angels. What Domiel feared had come true, but not because humans and angels were coexisting. The nightmare that had unfolded was Domiel's own doing.

I clenched my jaw and wondered why Father hadn't intervened. If He had a plan, He had not shared it with us, leaving us to deal with the aftermath on our own. Pandemonium surrounded us, with buildings burning, smoke filling the air, and people panicking. The responsibility weighed heavily on us, and we were compelled to make quick decisions independently and had to trust our instincts.

Theo, Willow, Annalise, and Dahlia were waiting at the garage entrance as we pulled up. As they climbed into the backseat, Annalise's eyes briefly met mine. An expression of worry flashed across her face. I gave her a reassuring nod, letting her know everything would be okay. She mouthed the words, *Thank you.* She had a right to be concerned. As much as I wanted to take away her uncertainty, I could not, but being at home might help.

Tension was evident in the Hummer as everyone settled in, lost in their own thoughts. Theo clenched his hands, and Willow stared out the window with her fingers tapping nervously on her knee. Dahlia, always the calmest among us, closed her eyes and centered on herself. Backing out of the garage, I turned my attention to the road.

As I drove down the dark streets, Willow asked, breaking the silence, "Why are all the lights out?" Her voice trailed off as she added, "I hope we're going to be okay."

I calmly said, "The power grid must have taken a hit. Don't worry. Our house has a backup generator. We'll be fine."

Chapter 10

Only the hum of the Hummer's engine interrupted the eerie drive through the darkened streets. Each turn revealed more shadowy houses barely visible against the night sky. The glow of our porch lights acted as a beacon as I approached our home. Pulling into the driveway, the Hummer's headlights lit up the front yard, and the old oak tree spread out its branches over the house like protective arms.

A sense of calm washed over me once I turned off the engine and stepped into the cool night air. Willow sighed with relief as light spilled onto our porch. Jahoel, Dahlia, and I followed Annalise as she led Willow and Theo to the front door. Stepping inside, the scent of lavender welcomed us, a stark contrast to the acrid smell of smoke still clinging to our clothes.

"We all need a shower and a change of clothes," Annalise said before pointing toward the hallway. "There are three bedrooms down the hall, each with its own bathroom. There's also a guest bathroom as well. All bathrooms have a linen closet stacked with towels and toiletries," she added.

Dahila wrinkled her nose as she sniffed her jacket. "I think we should toss our clothes. They aren't worth salvaging."

Annalise nodded. "Good point. I'll get everyone trash bags so they can dispose of their clothes."

"And I'll grab sweats for everyone to change into," I offered. My gaze fixed on Theo and Willow as I shook my head. "I'm not sure what we have will fit either of you."

"We can cut the sweats and make the arms and legs fit them," Annalise suggested.

"An excellent idea."

As I ran into our bedroom, I grabbed four pairs of sweats from the closet and returned with a full armload of clothes. Annalise cut the fabric to fit Theo and Willow, while Dahila and Jahoel took theirs.

Annalise held up a pair of sweatpants and T-shirts in front of Theo and Willow, gauging the amount of fabric she had cut off. "Perfect," she replied, and then distributed trash bags to everyone. She led Willow, Theo, and Dahlia to their rooms. I escorted Jahoel to the guest bathroom before returning to our room.

As soon as I entered the bathroom, I stripped off my clothes and threw them into the trash bag. I let the hot water wash away the stench of the night as I stood under the showerhead.

Annalise walked into the bathroom, shed her clothes into a trash bag, and joined me in the shower. Her eyes searched mine for answers I couldn't give. Tears welled up in her eyes as she held her head in her hands. I wrapped my arms around her, and she latched onto me. Even with the hot water and steam surrounding her, she shivered. Exhausted, we sat down on the shower bench, listening to the constant patter of water against the tiles. As her sobs subsided, she took deep, uneven breaths.

I whispered, "We're safe now."

A disbelieving look came over her face. "How could He allow such a thing to happen?" she asked.

"To be honest, I don't know."

After brushing a wet strand of hair away from her face, I kissed her. Her eyes closed as she leaned into my touch. A moment of pleasure passed between us as her lips caressed mine. A tingle of anticipation swept over our skin as we grew closer to each other. The softness of her skin against mine felt warm and moist as our hearts raced. A fervent desire gripped me as she straddled me and guided me inside her. No matter what horrors lay ahead, each touch, each kiss were silent promises that we would survive together. We held onto each other, finding strength in our vulnerability as we made love. For the first time that night, a glimmer of hope pierced the darkness.

After showering, we took our time drying off each other with adoration and tenderness. Steam lingered in the air as I wrapped the towel snugly around her shoulders, brushing a kiss across her forehead. Her eyes were calmer but still haunted by the night's events. Both Annalise and I dressed in sweatpants and hoodies. We shared one more kiss before joining the others.

Our family gathered around the island in the kitchen, the heart of our home. We designed our modern kitchen with gray-blue cabinets, stainless steel appliances, white quartz countertops, and dark wood plank floors. Three pendant lights elegantly hung above the island, bathing the group in a warm glow. Theo and Willow sat on bar stools. Jahoel and Dahlia stood behind them.

Annalise asked, "Who's hungry?" as we approached the gathering.

"Me!" Theo called out, raising his hand.

Willow's expression was less animated when she said, "I'm hungry too."

Annalise opened the lower cabinet door to reveal an array of stainless-steel pots and pans and selected a large pot. It gleamed under the kitchen lights as she carried the pot over to the pot filler. "How about homemade mac and cheese and tomato salad?" she asked, directing her question more toward the children.

Willow's previously reserved demeanor gave way to excitement, and her face lit up at the suggestion. "I love mac and cheese!"

"She'd eat it every day if she could," Theo teased.

"There's nothing better than mac and cheese," Annalise agreed. "Who wants to help with grating cheese and making breadcrumbs?"

"Me," Willow said, jumping out of her chair and running over to Annalise.

"I can help, too," Theo offered, joining his sister.

"Let's gather all the ingredients and put them on the island. We need macaroni, milk, butter, flour, cheddar cheese, breadcrumbs, crackers, salt, and pepper, and a baking dish. Where shall we find those?"

"The refrigerator," Willow replied.

"The pantry," Theo added.

"You're both right. Willow, why don't you get the items out of the refrigerator, and Theo, there's a walk-in pantry right through that door where you can collect the items you'll need."

My heart swelled with pride as I watched Annalise patiently guide Willow and Theo through the simple tasks, her gentle voice soothing their frayed nerves. She handed Willow the grater and showed her the best way to hold the cheese while she explained to Theo how to make the perfect breadcrumbs. The kitchen was suddenly filled with laughter and the clinking of pots and kitchen gadgets—a temporary refuge from the chaos outside.

"You're amazing," I whispered to Annalise before kissing her.

Theo theatrically pretended to gag, sticking out his tongue and scrunching his nose. Willow, on the other hand, peeked through her fingers, a mischievous grin spreading across her face. "Eww. You two are so embarrassing," she giggled.

An amused twinkle appeared in Annalise's eyes.

As I ruffled Theo's hair, I teased, "You'll understand when you're older."

"All right, team, let's focus!" As the kids eagerly resumed their tasks, Annalise declared, "We've got some mac and cheese to make."

Theo continued to crush crackers for the breadcrumbs while Willow grated cheese. The aroma of freshly grated cheese and butter melting in the pan filled the air, leaving my mouth watering. I glanced back at the kitchen one last time, taking in the sight of Annalise and the kids working together before motioning for Jahoel and Dahlia to follow me into the living room. Within its walls, I said, "We need to come up with a strategy. What happened at the church, and where did Father and our siblings disappear to?"

With his arms crossed, Jahoel said, "Let's start by stating everything we know."

Dahlia stared at him intently, her eyebrows furrowed. "Well, first, I think Father and our brothers and sisters are somewhere inside that old church."

"What makes you think that?" Jahoel posed.

"Just a gut feeling."

"Then we should go back there and look for clues," Jahoel suggested.

"I believe that's a futile attempt," I stated in frustration. "We were in that church, remember? Wouldn't we have seen clues? Also, regardless of what Theo and Willow said about their mother, I need to find her. She has to know that their father died."

"I already did," Dahlia said with a somber expression.

"You found her?" I asked.

"Yes."

"Are you sure that was their mother?"

"Azrael, I'm sure. She's dead."

My jaw dropped in disbelief. "Dead?"

"I used a strand of Willow's hair and channeled my angelic powers to search for their mother. I traced the ethereal connection between the hair and its source." Dahlia's voice grew hushed as she continued. "It led me to a grave. Their mother died three years ago. There are no other living relatives. It's just Theo and Willow now."

"We need to tell them," I said as I glanced toward the kitchen.

"I agreed. They deserve the truth," Dahlia said.

Jahoel placed a hand on my shoulder, his eyes filled with empathy. "Not yet," he protested. "First, we must focus on finding Father and fixing this mess."

Theo and Willow's circumstances occupied my thoughts; Jahoel's desire to make things right diminished. I wondered about their future without a mother or father. Would they stay together or would the foster care system split them apart? They needed love and a stable home, especially now. If we adopted them, Father could make it happen by circumventing all the red tape. Jahoel's voice intruded on my thoughts.

"I vote we go back to the church and take a look around. Azrael, do you agree?"

"We could, but given its state after the destruction, it's a long shot we'll find anything."

"There might be hidden passages or chambers we don't know about," Jahoel pointed out. "Time is crucial as Father has not responded to my mental messages. His silence is unlike Him, and it worries me, but I refuse to believe Father would abandon us now," he said with a curt nod.

Dahlia concurred. "My messages to both Father and Mother have also gone unanswered. His absence is unsettling and frightening. Mother left before anything happened, so why isn't she responding? It's not like them to disregard our attempts to contact them. None of this makes sense."

The fact that I had spent so many years on Earth, unaware of my origins, was likely the reason I had never sent a mental message to my Father. Nevertheless, I was capable of communicating now. Closing my eyes, I breathed deeply and focused on the divine energy that once flowed so effortlessly through me. "Father," I whispered in my head, "I need your guidance now more than ever. Please show us the way." As I opened my eyes, they fell on Annalise.

She wiped her hands on a dish towel as she said, "The mac and cheese is cooking, and Theo and Willow are watching TV in the family room." Her normally bright eyes grew apprehensive as they bounced between Jahoel, Dahlia, and me. "Did something happen?"

"Father's sudden disappearance has left us all shaken," I explained. "Jahoel thinks there might be clues or hidden passages in the Cathedral of Promise that could lead us to Him."

Her face paled, and she swallowed visibly. "You're going back there? Are you sure that's wise? After all those blasts, wouldn't the structure be unsafe?"

"It's risky given its current state, but it's the best lead we have right now," Jahoel conveyed. "The church might hold the answers to finding Father, and if there's even a small chance, we must try. Fear cannot paralyze us."

She stared at him for several moments before turning toward me. "It sounds like your minds are made up. Just promise me you'll be careful."

"We'll take every precaution," Dahlia assured, placing a caring hand on Annalise's shoulder.

"What should I tell Theo and Willow?" Annalise asked.

"We needed to leave to address a pressing matter," I proposed. "Reassure them that we'll be back soon, and everything will be okay."

Annalise nodded, yet unease flashed across her in her eyes.

"There's more." I pulled her aside and said, "Dahlia found out that Theo and Willow's mother passed away three years ago. They have no other family members. I was thinking we could adopt them, but if you don't agree with me, we can—"

She cut me off as her eyes widened in surprise. "Those poor kids. We absolutely need to give them a stable home, especially now."

"Then you're in agreement with me?"

"Yes, of course."

"I love you," I said as I hugged her tightly. "We'll get through this. For Father, for Theo and Willow, and for our own peace of mind."

"I love you, too." I heard her breath catch as she whispered, "Just promise me you'll stay safe and return to us."

I pulled back and looked into her hope-filled eyes. "I promise."

Chapter 11

An eerie silence greeted us as we entered the church. Wood, glass, and plaster littered the natural stone floor. Moonlight passed through the broken windows, illuminating the dust floating in the air. The altar stood untouched, a stark contrast to the surrounding rubble in the rest of the church. Among the overturned pews, scattered hymnbooks, and debris, there were no signs showing where our Father might be.

"Do you see any doors that might lead to passageways?" Jahoel inquired, his gaze scanning the room.

"Having been in this church many times, I know Father Logan has an office through that door in the far right-hand corner. Maybe his office has access to other areas within the church."

Dahlia headed toward the back of the church, saying, "We should check."

"That's his private office. We'd be trespassing."

"We're trespassing now."

"No," I argued. "We're in the church, which welcomes everyone."

"Desperate times call for desperate measures," Jahoel said, siding with Dahlia.

"You're welcome to stay here, but I'm looking." She approached his office door without waiting for a response.

After struggling with my conscience, I reluctantly followed Jahoel and Dahlia. Inviting us to explore its secrets, the door was slightly ajar. Upon entering, a faint smell of incense and old books filled the room. As I surveyed the dimly lit room, I was filled with curiosity. A large, wooden desk stood in the center, cluttered with papers. A pair of towering bookshelves stood on either side. After opening a second door next to the bookcase, Jahoel discovered a bathroom. He and Dahlia sighed together.

There was something about the bookcase that caught my attention. Among the rows of dust-covered books, one seemed out of place. The worn spine of the book tilted to one side. As I tugged gently on the book, the entire bookcase shifted, revealing a passageway. "I think I've found something."

Jahoel peeked inside and announced, "It leads to a hallway. I'm going in."

He entered, and Dahlia and I followed.

As we walked down a narrow corridor filled with cobwebs, our footsteps echoed on the concrete floor. At the end, we found a spacious chamber filled with ancient relics, scrolls, and ornate artifacts, all bathed in golden light.

After picking up a scroll, Dahlia concluded, "Father Logan seems to be quite the collector."

"Or an investigator," I commented, scanning the shelves. My gaze fell upon a leather-bound journal on display inside a glass-enclosed cabinet.

Clearly frustrated, Jahoel remarked, "We cannot waste time with relics and scrolls. We must explore and see if there are other rooms. Perhaps there is a chapel or even a basement that could provide us with clues about Father's whereabouts."

Jahoel left the chamber and returned to the hallway. Dahlia followed him. I lingered over the journal, intrigued. Its leather binder shimmered in golden light, tempting me to open it and delve into its pages. Despite the allure of the unknown, I knew I had to catch up with them, and Jahoel was correct; time was crucial.

"Little brother," Domiel whispered behind me.

As I turned around, his fist collided with my temple. Sharp pain shot through my skull, and my legs buckled beneath me. Cold sweat laced my skin as I crumpled to the ground. I struggled to remain conscious, but my vision blurred, and every sound faded. Domiel loomed over me, and the last thing I saw was his cruel smile etched on his face.

My eyes popped open as intense pain swept over me. It was as if I couldn't move, and I had lost my strength. Metal chains coiled around me, trapping me in a chair. The flickering ceiling lights created a strobe light effect on rusted machinery, broken crates, and racks of towering shelves. A drip of water echoing in the distance was the only sound. It was like an abandoned warehouse.

The light from a flashlight was shining directly into my eyes as a man approached me. Squinting, I tried to discern a silhouette.

"At last, you're awake," Domiel said as he lowered the flashlight.

Through clenched teeth, I spat, "You sucker punched me, and now I'm chained to a chair! Why?"

Domiel smirked. "Those aren't just any chains. They're forged by dwarves, and your shackling is necessary for us to communicate."

As I tried to move my hands, the chains tightened, making it worse. "You could have just asked me."

"You wouldn't have agreed."

"I brought you into my home. I spoke to Father on your behalf. Why would you resort to such drastic measures?"

The smirk on Domiel's face faded away as he leaned closer. "Father, Mother, Leilani, Orifiel, and Zaphkiel walked out of that church and left me behind. Azrael, you should have been my ally, but instead you chose Annalise over your own brother. Everything fell apart because you couldn't follow a simple plan."

I narrowed my eyes, trying to piece together his words, but the pain in my head made it difficult to concentrate. "What fell apart?"

"Throughout your immortal life, you remained in your corner of the world, releasing souls. The Angel of Death suited you perfectly. When Annalise passed away, you moped around, neglecting your duties. Father's heart broke to see His favorite son in such despair, so He transformed her into a human angel and sent her back to you." He groaned and closed his eyes. "However, Annalise's return caused more chaos than solace, transforming the once-confident Angel of Death into a shadow of his former self. Your decision to love her led Father to decide we all should live among humans."

"You don't decide to love someone. It just happens," I protested. "And I have no control over what Father wants to do or not do."

"Not directly but indirectly. Father watched you and Annalise. His idea arose from the two of you."

"Nevertheless, it's not my fault. Neither I, nor you, nor our siblings have a say in Father's decisions. I didn't start the war. You killed a man and left two children without a father because of your actions."

He firmly pressed a stiff finger into my chest. "It *was* you. The only reason I'm on Earth is because of what you did."

"I didn't ask you or force you to come here. I didn't even remember my past until you awakened my memories. When you told me about Father's plan and asked for my help, I agreed. Is this my token of gratitude, being shackled to a chair?"

"That's so typical of you. You never take responsibility for *your* actions! Your choices caused chaos to follow." His eyes bulged with rage as he yelled, "I lost everything because of your recklessness. Now it's time for you to step up and fix what you've caused."

As I stared at his wild, frenzied expression, I couldn't shake the feeling that something ominous lurked behind that intense gaze. This wasn't the Domiel I knew. Madness and irrationality took the place of reason and logic. No matter what I said, I feared he wouldn't listen. I found myself trapped, helpless, and alone with him.

"Did you hear what I said?" Impatience laced his tone as he shouted my name. "Azrael!"

The dryness of my throat prevented any words from forming.

Tension rippled through his jaw, and darkness filled his eyes. An animalistic growl raced past his lips as he slammed his fist into my face. My head jerked backward as blood gushed out of my nose. A throbbing, stinging ache burrowed itself into my right cheekbone, lighting my face on fire. With my right eye swollen shut, my left struggled to compensate as Domiel's image blurred before me.

Grabbing my shirt and pulling me close, his voice cracked as he said, "Azrael, I trusted you. Why did you betray me?"

Pain and confusion delayed my response. "Domiel, I—I don't—don't know what you're talking about," I stammered.

He tightened his grip on me as he chided, "You were the only one who knew what I wanted."

I forced my hands apart, trying to free them, but the metal chains tightened with relentless and calculated malice as if trying to stop me. I couldn't give up. I had to fight. I had to keep my promise to Annalise.

Spit flew from his mouth as he screamed, "Say something!"

Trying to recall any act of betrayal I'd committed, panic rose in my chest. "I didn't betray you," I blurted out.

As his eyes grew darker and more insane, I knew I'd said the wrong thing. He kicked the chair with force, sending both me and the chair flying across the room. The chair split in half on impact. I landed hard on the cold concrete floor, the sharp edges of the broken chair penetrating deeply into my flesh. Fresh agony radiated through my body, but adrenaline kept me focused. As I crawled away, the chains clinked ominously on the floor, and warm, sticky blood oozed from my wounds, trailing after me.

Domiel's foot collided with my ribs, and the cracking of my bones filled my ears. He kicked me again, striking my stomach. Bright red blood spurted from my mouth, spraying the floor. I moaned as I wrapped my arms around my torso, holding myself together as my body collapsed in on itself. Every breath pierced my chest with crippling pain. Choking on my own blood, I pleaded, "Stop."

He grabbed my neck and showed no mercy, his crushing grip cutting off oxygen. Struggling for air, I clawed at his hands. A strangled "please" passed my lips.

"Domiel, enough!" Father commanded with authority.

Domiel refused to obey. His grasp was relentless as his fingers squeezed my throat. My vision dimmed, further distorting my perception.

"Release him now or face my wrath," Father warned.

Domiel's hands fell to his sides. Air flooded my lungs, then sharp, relentless pain raged inside me, gripping my ribs with every inhale. My muscles constricted involuntarily, and a cold sweat formed on my forehead.

"Unchain Azrael at once," Father ordered. "Should I use this rare metal on you as well, Domiel, and fill you with its toxins? An eye for an eye?"

A flurry of footsteps echoed in my ears. Jahoel appeared beside me. Gloves covered his hands as he unwound the chains. "Everything will be alright," he assured.

The pain sucked the life out of me. My chest seemed to cave, like a heavy weight pressing down on it. As I lay on the concrete floor, my arms limp at my sides, I labored to breathe. The ache swiftly penetrated my head, pounding like an imminent explosion. Despite Jahoel's comforting words, I feared it wouldn't be okay.

He gently lifted my head and cradled it in his hands as he turned to Father. "Azrael doesn't look well. He needs medical attention. His breathing is shallow, and his skin is a disturbing shade of gray. We must act quickly before the toxin spreads," he exclaimed.

"See that he receives the aid he requires," Father said. "I will join you once I have dealt with Domiel."

After picking me up, Jahoel ran out of the building. His wings spread as he soared upward, lifting us higher in the night sky. The wind rushed past us, its cool touch soothing the burning pain. I fluttered in and out of consciousness, thankful for the unconscious moments free of pain. In front of an emergency room, Jahoel descended, folding his wings neatly against his back. "Stay with me, Azrael," he urged.

Within moments, doors whooshed open, blaring fluorescent lights hit my left eye, and the smell of sterile antiseptic filled the room. Jahoel placed me in a chair and shouted, "My brother needs help."

My blurred gaze drifted up finding his eyes, and I murmured, "Go get Annalise. I need her."

"Dr. Marshall, we have a penetrating trauma," someone yelled.

An army of nurses in green shirts surrounded me. They laid me on a gurney and rolled me into a room filled with machines, and the antiseptic smell intensified. Dr. Marshall, a tall man with sharp features, stood over me, examining the pieces of wood protruding from my body. A nurse hooked me up to the monitor, and my steady heartbeat lit up, pulsing up and down on the screen.

The cold metal of Dr. Marshall's stethoscope sent shivers through me. His gloved hands rolled me onto my side, and I winced as he pressed gently on my ribs, nose, and cheek. As he lifted my right eyelid and waved a penlight over it, a bright beam of light swept across my eye.

"There is a subconjunctival hemorrhage, but the pupil remains responsive. Get a head CT, CBC, and abdominal scan," he ordered.

When a needle punctured my arm, it burned, and I closed my eyes. The gurney shifted forward, and then I was in motion as they wheeled me out of the room. I called out to Jahoel and once again begged him to get Annalise.

As the ceiling tiles rushed past me, the overhead lights blurred into streaks. Every jolt of the gurney sent a fresh wave of pain through my body, but my mind clung to Annalise. The nurse turned a corner and wheeled me into a bright, white room. The harsh fluorescent light shone over a large tubular machine. Its circular opening reminded me of a portal into another world. They lifted me off the gurney and placed me on the table.

A technician instructed me to remain still as the machine buzzed and circled around me. The humming and beeping surrounded me for several minutes as I tried to ignore the feeling of claustrophobic isolation. Annalise's smile filled my mind as I lay there. Through the intercom, the technician assured me that it would soon end. The sounds grew faint, and the lights dimmed as the machine whirled to a stop.

They transferred me back to the gurney and wheeled me into a different room. My gaze focused on a table in the center of the room, surrounded by medical staff wearing masks and green scrubs. Large, circular lights shined directly on the table, and behind the table were more beeping machines and blinking monitors. The fluorescent lights glowed on an array of surgical instruments: scalpels, forceps, scissors, retractors, and some I didn't recognize. I was certain I was in an operating room. Two nurses, their faces covered in masks, lifted me onto the surgical table, the cool metal causing me to shiver. Another masked person approached and said, "Hello, Azrael. I'm Dr. Silman, your surgeon. My team and I will remove the pieces of wood from your body. In no time we will have you in recovery." He gestured toward a man sitting next to one of the machines. "This is Dr. Nash, your anesthesiologist."

Dr. Nash nodded at me before turning to a woman standing next to him. "Nurse Romeno will start your IV."

"I'm going to numb your hand before inserting your IV," she said in a gentle tone. "You won't feel a thing."

My mind raced with questions, wondering how my immortal body would react to anesthesia. Would it simply pass through me, leaving me conscious throughout the surgery? Or would I fall unconscious as the anesthesia mixed with the toxins coursing through my veins?

As Nurse Romeno swabbed my hand, I hoped for the latter. She inserted the needle, causing a fleeting sting and spreading a warm sensation throughout my body.

Dr. Nash leaned over me, his voice calm and reassuring. "You'll start to feel drowsy. Just focus on relaxing."

I nodded, my eyelids growing heavier, unable to resist the urge to close. As the hum of the machines faded into the background, I slipped deeper into unconsciousness. My last coherent thought was of Annalise before I surrendered to the anesthesia.

When my eyes fluttered open, it seemed as if only minutes had passed since Dr. Nash told me I would feel sleepy. As I scanned the room, something seemed off. Its concrete floors stretched for miles, and its gray walls reached beyond its high ceilings. As I lay on the operating table, unable to move, I was alone. My arms and legs felt heavy. My breathing was the only sound. What happened to everyone? Had Dr. Silman completed my surgery? Why was I alone? Why couldn't I move? No explanation made sense.

A golden light crossed the table and embraced me in comforting warmth. As soon as I recognized my Father's olive-green eyes, I realized it was more than just light. A luminescent aura swirled from his hands as he held them over my body. "Lie still, Azrael, while I flush away the toxins from your body."

I lay motionless, uncertain if I was dreaming or under anesthesia. "Father?" I called. "Are you really here, or is this a side effect of the anesthesia?"

"I am here with you, my son," He said as he gently squeezed my shoulder.

"What happened? Where is everyone? I don't understand."

"You are still in surgery. Your doctors have no understanding of celestial toxins and will not heal you with their treatment.

I have created a barrier around us that is invisible to the human eye, allowing me to draw out the poison without interference and allowing you to heal from your surgery."

A gentle tugging sensation spread through my body as grayish particles oozed from my skin. Father seized them, sent them spiraling upward before dissolving them into nothingness, and released me from the weight that bound my body. I could move again. His love radiated through me as I stared into His eyes.

"It is done," He said and leaned over to kiss my forehead. "There is more to discuss. I'll see you in recovery."

As the room darkened and the muted gray walls faded away, I fell into a dreamless sleep.

The next time I opened my eyes, I was lying in a hospital bed with a heated blanket covering me. The monitor next to the bed displayed my heartbeat. An IV hung overhead, slowly dripping clear fluid into my veins. Looking around, I realized I could see with both eyes. My gaze landed on Annalise sitting by my bedside and holding my hand, my heartbeat spiked, and tears filled my eyes. Father and Jahoel sat on a bench at the back of the room.

"I was so worried about you, Clay," Annalise said softly as she squeezed my hand.

I looked away, avoiding her gaze. I shifted uncomfortably, feeling a flush of shame creep up my neck. As I met her eyes, I said, "I apologize for breaking my promise."

"What's important is that you're safe now," she said, in her tender, warm voice. "How are you feeling?"

Her gentle demeanor eased my tension, allowing me to breathe easier. "I feel better now that you're here," I replied, using my free hand to touch her face.

She blinked tears from her eyes and smiled once more before glancing back at Father and Jahoel, who nodded supportively.

Dr. Silman interrupted our moment by entering the room and mimicking Annalise's question. "How are you feeling?"

Pushing my body upward into a sitting position, I winced and clenched my jaw, waiting for the pain to subside. Seeing my discomfort, Annalise squeezed my hand again, offering silent support. After a moment, I responded. "I can see out of both eyes, so I think the swelling has gone down. My ribs, stomach, and back are pretty sore."

Dr. Silman nodded, seemingly unconcerned about my pain. "On the right side of your face and ribcage, you suffered a fractured cheekbone and three broken ribs. I removed all the wood from your stomach and back and cleaned up the splinters. Some discomfort is normal, but it shouldn't be excessive," he explained. "For the next few weeks, it's important to rest and take it easy. You'll stay on antibiotics and pain medication during that time to promote healing."

"When can I go home?" I asked.

He took a moment to review my chart before saying, "We'll closely monitor your progress, and I should have an answer for you soon, but you're on your way to recovery."

Father extended His hand to Dr. Silman. "Thank you, Dr. Silman, for taking care of my son."

Dr. Silman shook His hand and assured Him, "Azrael will be back on his feet in no time. We'll have a nurse check on him regularly and adjust his medications as needed." He nodded and then left the room.

Father turned to Jahoel and asked, "Jahoel, could you please give me a moment alone with Azrael and Annalise?"

Jahoel rose to his feet as he answered, "Of course." He stopped at my bedside and squeezed my shoulder before leaving.

"I am very proud of you, Azrael. You have shown incredible strength and resilience throughout this situation," Father said softly, pulling a chair closer to my bedside. As He continued, His voice deepened with sadness. "Domiel's reckless behavior not only hurts you but also the human world, and he must take responsibility for his actions and learn from his mistakes. Thus, he will serve as the Angel of Death in your place."

The weight of my Father's words settled heavily on my chest. A mix of emotions surged within me—disbelief, doubt, and apprehension. "Did I do something wrong, Father?" I asked, my voice strained.

Putting His hand over mine, He said, "You did nothing wrong, Azrael. This is not punishment for you, but a necessary path to Domiel's growth. Domiel must soften his heart. Sending humans into the afterlife should alter his view of mankind."

"What will my role be?"

"You and Annalise are embarking on a new journey. Your family will soon expand, and you also have Willow and Theo to consider. I'm aware you both want to adopt them, so I have coordinated with angels on Earth to carry out those plans. Parenting demands presence and attention, which makes constant travel impossible. Your family must now be the center of your focus."

My stomach knotted up with anxiety as I tried to understand His words. It terrified me to think I might lose my immortality, and I also feared Annalise would lose hers. What would it mean to live a life with an endpoint, to experience the passage of time as a mortal does? How would Annalise cope with such a drastic change? "Father, I don't understand what you mean. Will I lose my immortality? Does Annalise suffer the same fate?"

"My dear son, you and Annalise are immortal angels and will forever be so. It has always been your dream to become an angel of mercy. The opportunity has now arisen for you to achieve your dream. In times of need, those seeking your mercy will turn to you for assistance. Nevertheless, Willow, Theo, and your unborn twins must take precedence."

As the word slammed into my head, I went blank. I opened my mouth, but no words emerged. Slowly, I turned my head to look at Annalise, whose wide-eyed expression mirrored mine. I turned back to my Father and asked, "Twins?"

Before He could respond, Annalise blurted out, "Am I pregnant?"

Father replied, "Yes."

"But how?" Annalise stammered, "I died, ascended to Heaven, and returned as an angel."

"All truths. I brought you back to life—an immortal life—to live on Earth with my son." His eyes darted between us. "Azrael has benefited from your influence, just as you have benefited from him. There is no limit to your love for each other. Like humans, you both possess the capability of procreation. In contrast to humans, though, you and Azrael have supernatural gifts, are ageless, and heal quickly. Parenthood is a blessing for both of you."

My Father's words shook my soul, and my eyes filled with tears. For centuries, my purpose was to end life, not create it. Being a father was something I never thought possible. I had received the most precious gift, but did Annalise share my sentiments? I turned my gaze toward her. Her wide-eyed, stunned expression remained fixed on her face. Her hands trembled slightly as she placed them over her stomach, as if trying to feel life growing inside her. I reached for her hand, feeling the warmth and softness of her skin against mine. "Annalise, I know this is unexpected, but I promise we'll make it work."

Softly gasping, she stared at the floor as a shock passed through her body. After a moment, she met my gaze, whispering, "This is beyond what I could have imagined." As she looked at my Father, she again asked, "Are you sure?"

"A doctor will confirm my words within four months. I am sorry to be so blunt, but Annalise, you will soon feel nauseated and fatigued. Both you and Azrael will become consumed with fear and believe disease has returned. Therefore, I chose to reveal your pregnancy now to prevent unnecessary grief and worry later on."

"I'm completely overwhelmed and terrified at the thought of being a mother. In my short, sick life, my own mother taught me two things: to be overly cautious and protective. I'm still getting used to the idea of being a mom to Theo and Willow, and now I'm having twins. I feel like my angelic life has thrown me into a whirlwind of major responsibilities all at once, and I wonder if I'm ready for these monumental shifts."

As her expression changed from shock to uncertainty, I began to worry that this might be too much for her to handle.

Taking her hands, my Father said, "Annalise, you're strong, compassionate, and caring. Never doubt your abilities. Look at how you cared for Willow and Theo during their father's devastating death."

She looked at me, her eyes searching for answers. I took a deep breath, trying to steady my own nerves as I smiled at her.

Gently squeezing her hand, I said, "You're going to be an amazing mother."

"You both seem so certain. I wish I had your confidence."

"If this is not something you want," I said quietly, "I will support whatever decision you make."

Her gaze softened, and a small smile formed on her lips. "Clay," she said, her voice full of emotion. "No matter how scared I am, I want to have these children with you."

As she embraced me, I kissed her softly, and my pulse accelerated, displaying my feelings on the monitor.

A knock at the door pulled us apart. Jahoel stood hesitantly at the doorway, his hand poised to knock again. Looking into my hospital room, he asked softly, "Is it okay if I come back in?"

Father waved him forward. "Come in, Jahoel."

He entered my hospital room with a strong stride. "I spoke with Dahlia. Willow and Theo asked when Clay would be home." Jahoel pressed his lips together after uttering the name and stared at me. "I don't understand why you don't use your given name."

"I suggested Clay," Annalise said. "It's more appropriate than Death," she continued, her voice firm but gentle.

In an effort to explain, I said, "Changing from Death to Clay was like shedding an old skin." As Jahoel looked at me defiantly, I added, "I called myself Death, not Azrael."

In response, Jahoel shrugged, but his expression confirmed he disagreed. "I owe Dahlia a response. Willow and Theo are worried, and they want to visit."

Father said, "Clay suits you."

Annalise nodded. "I agree."

Jahoel scowled. "Fine. What should I tell Dahlia?"

"The heaviness in my body has decreased, but Dr. Silman will not commit to a date." As I demonstrated, I slowly lifted my arm, and even though it trembled a bit, I lifted a leg more steadily. Despite the beads of sweat forming on my forehead, I laughed. "It's not much, but it's progress."

In an encouraging tone, Father replied, "Yes, it is. Your strength and mobility will continue to improve now that the poison has left your system."

"I'll tell Dahlia you're making progress, but the kids will want to see it for themselves."

"Wait," Annalise interrupted. "He was poisoned?" She turned to me, her eyes searching my face for confirmation. "You were poisoned?"

As I looked into her eyes, I felt shame for what Domiel did, even though it was his fault, not mine. "He chained me to a chair," I said, twisting the covers between my hands. "Domiel specifically laced the chains with celestial poison. His plan was to weaken me and prevent me from escaping," I explained, feeling the weight of the memory pressing down on me.

She clenched her fists as her expression shifted from shock to anger. "How could he do such a thing?" Before anyone could reply, she turned toward my Father and asked, "Why would you want him to replace Clay? He should have nothing to do with humans, especially releasing their souls!"

Jahoel nodded slowly, acknowledging the truth in Annalise's words. "She's got a point."

Though uncertainty filled me, I didn't let it show through my words. "Perhaps I should talk to him. He thinks that I betrayed him. Maybe he's holding onto a misunderstanding or a disagreement we had in the past."

"He's jealous and bitter," Annalise snapped back. "You can't trust him. Who knows what he'll try this time around?"

"But he's my brother." I replied. "I can't turn my back on him. We once shared an unbreakable bond. I must have done something to make him feel this way."

With a sigh, she shook her head. "Clay, listen to yourself."

My Father held up His hands and halted our discussion. "I believe I have something to do with all of this. My fascination with angels interacting with humans began when you met Annalise. When I proposed their coexistence, Domiel became enraged and sought allies to prevent it from happening. He expected you to be one of his greatest allies, but reality was quite different. Domiel planned out the celestial earthquakes, the terrorizing of humans, and the strategy to win."

Jahoel stepped forward and declared, "I will temporarily assume the role of Angel of Death and take on the burden of guiding souls until Father can repair the rift between Domiel and humans."

"Jahoel, I commend your commitment. However, I often call upon you and Dahlia. I do agree Annalise has a valid point. I will replace Azrael with another suitable individual."

Annalise replied, "Thank you," and then winked at me as though she'd won her point.

In response to her smug expression, I crossed my arms and raised an eyebrow.

Her eyes twinkled with mischief as she teased, "That look on your face is priceless."

Shaking my head, I replied, "Is that so?"

"Yes," she said and kissed my cheek.

"It's been a long day, and you need to rest." Father said, "And I need to deal with Domiel." His nod signaled Jahoel. "I would appreciate your help with Domiel. Are you available to come with me?"

"Of course, Father."

My Father leaned over and kissed my cheek. "You're in excellent hands with Annalise. I'll check in tomorrow."

"I would like to stay with Clay at the hospital tonight. Could Dahlia stay with Willow and Theo?" Annalise asked.

Jahoel nodded. "She will."

Annalise hugged Jahoel and then my Father, saying, "Thank you both."

A spark of desire ignited within me as I watched her effortlessly bond with my family. As I lay in the hospital bed, with the sterile walls and beeping machines, her smile made everything feel more like home. Despite the chaos and uncertainty surrounding us, I knew Annalise would always be there for me.

Father and Jahoel waved as they stepped through the doorway. A soft glow surrounded them as they slowly faded into shimmering light.

With a reassuring squeeze of my hand, Annalise left the room, saying, "I'll be right back. I'm going to check on getting a cot for the room."

Without her, the room felt empty, but I knew she would return, bringing her warmth and comfort. The hum of the machines reminded me of my current situation. I needed to change that. Throwing the covers aside, I sat on the edge of the bed and lifted my left leg, forcing it over the bedside. Beads of sweat formed on my brow as I did the same with my right leg. After placing both feet on the floor, I used my hands to push myself upward.

Trembling uncontrollably, I raised myself about two inches off the bed before my muscles failed to support me, and I plopped back down. I was breathless, and my heartbeat surged on the monitor. Frustration welled inside me, but I refused to give up.

I gripped the bed rails, feeling the cool metal press against my palms. My determination overshadowed my fatigue, urging me to continue. I inhaled deeply and exhaled slowly, preparing for another attempt. With a surge of strength, I rose into an upright position. Feeling the strain in my legs, I planted my feet firmly on the tile floor and stood a little taller. Sweat trickled into my eyes as I stood there, clutching the bed rail like it was my lifeline. My legs wobbled beneath me, but I remained standing. Although I had achieved victory, I was afraid to take a step forward.

As the door opened, Annalise rushed to my side with a gasp. "Clay, what are you doing?" She glanced at the monitor, noting the erratic beeping that echoed my heartbeat. She hovered protectively around me, ready to catch me. "You should have called for help or waited for me to return. You could have fallen."

"I want to go home, Annalise. I want to be with you, the kids, and my family. I need to make progress because if I don't regain my strength, I'll remain trapped here. Until I can prove I can stand up and get around, Dr. Silman won't sign off on my release."

"Then, I'll help you. Lean on me," she said, slipping her arm around my waist and hooking my arm around her shoulders.

Holding tight to her, I slowly rose. Sweat soaked through my hospital gown. As my body shook, my legs threatened to collapse. She held her arm around me, keeping me steady. After stepping forward, I blew out several quick breaths. I took another step, and then another, until I stood in the center of the room. I could not go further because of the IV. Though I could have wheeled it along with me, exhaustion forced me back to bed.

Annalise gently dabbed my face with a towel, and she said with encouragement, "You're making progress. A little more each day, and you'll be home soon."

I smiled, attempting to ignore the overwhelming fatigue that weakened my entire being. "I just walked five steps, and I'm exhausted."

"I promise, it will get easier," she said softly.

Looking into her eyes, I nodded, but frustration gnawed at me. My muscles ached with every movement, a stark contrast to the strength I once took for granted. "I'm immortal. I shouldn't be in this position. Damn Domiel and his chains."

A look of empathy filled her eyes as she gazed at me. The gentle touch that she provided comforted me, even as I allowed my exasperation to overcome my resolve.

A nurse entered, wheeling in a cot for Annalise. After she set it up in the corner of the room, she came over to check my temperature and pulse, change out the IV bag, and give me my pain injection. "If you need anything, Mr. Bennett, just press the call button," she said as she laid the call button next to me.

"Thank you. I'll do that."

Annalise and I exchanged puzzled glances as soon as she left the room.

"Did she just call you Mr. Bennett?" Annalise asked, furrowing her brow.

Perplexed, I shrugged. "Perhaps the hospital had mistaken my records for someone else's, or maybe Jahoel or Father had orchestrated the entire situation. Most likely, it was Jahoel's doing.

He was the one who brought me into the hospital. He had to fill out paperwork, right?"

Laughing, she mused, "I feel like we're on some secret mission to uncover the truth. But we do need a last name, especially now that we're adopting." She glanced at her belly. "And having twins."

It had all happened so fast. Within days, our lives had completely changed. Becoming a father to four children filled me with joy and anxiety. This role of being a parent would carry more responsibility than anything I'd ever done throughout my entire existence. "The adoption is definitely going to require documents. Perhaps that's why the name was chosen." I frowned. "But my Father or Jahoel should have said something to us. We can ask them tomorrow." I took her hand. "I've been thinking."

A playful glint lit up her eyes as she teased, "That's never a good thing."

Laughing, I said, "You're right, I can get caught up in things. Though I believe I have a valid point about this. Despite Theo and Willow's hardship, should we assume they want us to be their parents? Should we ask them how they feel about us adopting them?"

She cocked her head as she processed my question. "I hadn't even considered that," she confessed. "I agree. We shouldn't assume what they want. We need to make sure they feel included in this process. We will ask them."

"Oh, and one more thing. We should be honest with them about our existence. It would strengthen our relationship with them and foster trust and understanding."

"I understand your point, but they're just kids," she pointed out. "Exposing them to such a complex reality could overwhelm them. They've already faced so much, and I'm afraid it could add unnecessary stress. I agree, though, that we should let them know

I am pregnant. They'll know that even though you and I are expecting our own children, we still want to adopt them."

While I saw her side, it felt wrong to hide the truth. I did not know much about children, but a 9- or 10-year-old seemed capable of understanding God and angels. The concept differed from the reality of our existence on Earth, however. Before I spoke, I tried to find the best words. "It may be difficult for them to comprehend, but they deserve honesty. Perhaps we can explain things gradually, starting with the basics and answering each question as it arises."

Her shoulders slumped as she sighed. "It's not just about understanding complex beings," she insisted. "Trauma has affected them, and they are still healing. We need to create a safe environment for them first, where they feel loved and secure. Also, we have no idea what their religious beliefs are."

A flurry of thoughts raced through my mind as I stared at the determination etched into her face. Her argument had some merit. Neither of us knew anything about their lives. I admired Annalise's perspective, but I couldn't ignore the feeling that honesty was the best approach. I wondered if it was possible to strike a balance between protecting them and giving them the truth they deserved. "I appreciate your point, Annalise, but they will notice things, such as the fact that we don't age. Immortals stop aging once they reach adulthood. You stopped aging when your physical body died. Furthermore, my strength, gift, and, most importantly, the fact that my family is of heavenly persuasion, are all things they will eventually see. Most likely sooner than later."

Her eyes flickered upward as she pursed her lips. "Perhaps you're right."

"I suppose we could present a more nuanced version of the truth."

"That's definitely an option."

Chapter 12

Three days later, I entered our home, assisted by Jahoel and Annalise. Theo and Willow ran toward us, their footsteps tapping against the floor in the background. As they threw their arms around me and hugged me tightly, a pang of pain gripped me. I winced slightly but smiled, grateful for their eager affection. Their worried eyes met mine, searching for reassurance.

"You need to be careful. Clay is recovering," Annalise cautioned.

Theo loosened his grip, stepping back while Willow held on, her concern evident. "We missed you and were worried about you," she mumbled into my chest.

As I ruffled Theo's hair and squeezed Willow's shoulder, their joy encased me. "I'm thrilled to see you too, and I'm okay, Willow. I just need to take it easy and rest."

Jahoel chuckled and said, "Give Azrael some space to breathe, you two."

"Let's get you settled on the couch," Annalise said as she guided me into the living room. She arranged pillows behind my back, put my feet up on the ottoman, and tucked a blanket over my legs. "I'll make you some tea," she offered. Her gaze fell on Theo and Willow, who sat on either side of me. "The two of you can keep Clay company."

Upon entering the living room, Dahlia hugged me and said, "Welcome home, Azrael. How are you feeling?"

A sigh escaped my lips. "I'm worn out and sore. It's been a long few days." I squeezed her hands. "Thank you so much for taking care of Theo and Willow."

Dahlia smiled warmly and nodded. "You know I'm always here for you."

We hugged once more before letting go. "Father requested Jahoel and I stay here while you recuperate and watch over you, Annalise, and the children."

"We're here to help with anything you need," Jahoel pledged.

The feeling of satisfaction took hold of me as my family surrounded me in the familiarity of my home.

"I'm practically a teenager," Theo insisted, puffing out his chest with an exaggerated sense of importance.

With a wink, Dahlia said, "And you're a valiant warrior against under-the-bed monsters. Every night, Theo patrols the house with his trusty flashlight and fierce scowl. It's no wonder we feel safe," she added.

Willow smiled at Theo. "He's really good at it, too. When I get scared at night, he's always there to make sure I'm okay," she said as she showed off her bracelet. "He even made me a special monster-repelling charm bracelet from his stone collection."

Theo's eyes twinkled with delight. "No monster stands a chance against me!" he said, raising his imaginary sword high in the air, "I'll protect you all, even if it means staying up all night."

Jahoel settled into an armchair, nodding approvingly at Theo's antics. "You are a true hero, Theo."

Dahlia clapped her hands in admiration.

Taking in the praise, his cheeks flushed. Willow giggled as she spun her bracelet. I gave Theo a thumbs-up, affirming his role as the household's protector.

The aroma of honey, lemon, and Earl Grey tea teased my senses as Annalise stepped into the room. She handed me a steaming cup of tea. I sighed with contentment as I took a sip. Annalise beamed as she took in the sight of Theo and Willow snuggling up on either side of me. She settled into the oversized armchair opposite the sofa and tucked her legs beneath her as she cradled her own cup of tea between her hands.

Catching Annalise's gaze, I raised a brow, indicating I wanted to approach the subject of adoption, the twins, and the truth about us. I nodded slightly toward the others so that she understood. A flicker of recognition passed between us, signaling for me to proceed.

"Annalise and I wanted to talk about something with you two." I looked at Willow and Theo, directing my statement to them. "We hope you'll find it appealing. How do you feel about me and Annalise adopting you?"

Theo's brows furrowed, while Willow's lips curled into a cautious smile. Their startled expressions reflected a whirlwind of emotions as they contemplated the gravity of our offer. My pulse quickened with anticipation as I awaited a response.

Theo spoke first. "We don't really know either of you, but you've been very kind to us. It's a big decision, and Willow and I have talked about staying here. I told her that since you're all angels, and I believe your Dad is God, I think we'd be safe here."

After my eyes fluttered shut, they popped open wide, and I just stared. Annalise sat still and expressionless. Jahoel blinked rapidly before rising out of the chair but said nothing.

"What gave you the idea that we were angels?" Dahlia asked, folding her arms as she looked at Theo and Willow.

Theo smirked as he said, "You talk a lot in your sleep. We tried not to eavesdrop, but it's almost impossible not to, and your wings come out when you're dreaming. I've seen them a few times, and Willow has too."

Willow nodded in agreement, adding, "And sometimes there's a warm glow around you."

Annalise and I shared a surprised glance, realizing how perceptive the kids were and how much they had observed without us knowing. I was slightly amused. No matter how discreet we thought we were, nothing escaped their sharp gazes.

Dahila halfheartedly shrugged her shoulders as she said, "That's what happens when you sleep on a sofa bed in the family room."

As he chuckled, Jahoel reflected, "Well, it seems the secret's out, and I'm rather pleased that it's no longer necessary to conceal my wings."

As I found my voice, I clarified, "Jahoel, Dahlia, and I are siblings, and, yes, our Father *is* God. Annalise was once human; however, a terrible disease took her life, and I sent her to Heaven. My Father realized how much she meant to me and sent her back to Earth as a human angel to be by my side."

Theo's lips parted in awe, and Willow's cautious smile transformed into pure fascination. She whispered, "I knew you were special."

"And so are both you and Theo," I repeated.

A beam of pride filled Theo's eyes, while Willow's cheeks blushed brightly.

As I gazed at Theo and Willow, guilt overshadowed my joy. Domiel, my own brother, orchestrated the tragedy that left them orphaned, but I led Father to the church. I also played a part. If I had thought more carefully about the situation, I could have prevented it, but I trusted him as a brother. My actions had devastating consequences, but I never imagined his intentions could be so malicious. The burden of my decision weighed on my conscience.

In my heart, I vowed to make amends and protect Theo and Willow. "There's more to it," I said. "My brother, Domiel, caused the chaos at the church, killed your father, and tried to kill me." My emotions raged, and I clenched my hands as I admitted the truth. Theo and Willow could never experience such pain again. "Our Father hopes Domiel can find redemption, but he is dangerous at the moment, which is why Jahoel and Dahlia are watching over us."

Annalise got up from her chair and sat next to us on the sofa. She took Theo's hand, squeezing it gently. As she wrapped her other arm around Willow's shoulders, she pulled her into an embrace. Annalise spoke softly, her tone convincing. "We can never replace your father. I promise that if you allow us to be part of your family, we will love you, take care of you, and keep you safe."

Willow clasped her hand as she said, "I would like that."

Theo nodded. "Me too."

"Then it's settled," I said, uniting all three in a powerful hug.

Willow's eyes grew wide with excitement as she asked, "Would we get to decorate our bedrooms?"

Annalise laughed. "Of course."

"Annalise and I have more news to share." I nudged Annalise. "Tell them."

Annalise breathed deeply while resting her hand on her stomach, glancing around the room, meeting everyone's eyes as she revealed, "I'm pregnant. Clay and I are expecting twins."

Dahlia and Jahoel stared open-mouthed at each other. Uncertainty had replaced Jahoel's usual confidence, and Dahlia's hand instinctively flew to her mouth. Electric tension rippled between them in the air around them. Dahlia leaned toward Jahoel and whispered, "Twins?"

Theo's eyes lit up, and a huge grin spread across his face. He whooped with excitement and laughed out loud. "Wow, I guess I'll have to teach them all the cool things I know."

Willow bounced up and down. Her eyes sparkled as she clapped her hands together in delight. "I'm going to be the best big sister ever!" she exclaimed, her voice bubbling with glee. "I can't wait to show them all my favorite books. I'll read them stories and play games with them. I can help with everything."

"You two will be amazing siblings, and I can definitely use all your help," Annalise said, ruffling their hair and kissing them both on the cheek.

Looking around the room, I couldn't help but smile at the thought of my expanding family. I imagined laughter echoing through the halls and meals shared around the dining table. In such a short time, our family had grown from just the two of us to adding Theo and Willow, and now twins—a family of six. There was definitely a need for more space. My mind raced with possibilities: We could add an extension on the top of the house for Jahoel and Dahlia. While I was excited to embark on this new chapter, it was also a huge responsibility, one that I had no experience in.

Dahlia interrupted my thoughts. "Azrael, may Jahoel and I speak with you privately?" Her voice carried a hint of urgency, which was unusual for her.

Getting up slowly, I replied, "Of course."

In a flash, they swept me across the room, each grasping my arms as they did so. Jahoel looked over his shoulder, making sure no one had followed us. As we reached the far corner of the room, Dahlia loosened her grip on my arm and inquired, "She's pregnant?"

I furrowed my brow as I said, "Yes. Why am I repeating what Annalise already told you?"

Standing tall, Jahoel exuded authority. He stared into my eyes, asking firmly, "Is Father aware of this?"

My jaw clenched as frustration swelled inside me. It sounded more like a challenge than a question. As for my tone, I kept it civil. "I don't understand why that matters, but yes, He knows. In fact, it was Father who informed Annalise and me at the hospital."

"Do you not see the impact of a human angel procreating with the Angel of Death?" Jahoel looked at me with disbelief in his eyes. "The merging of these two beings could lead to unforeseen consequences, Azrael. A child born of such a union might possess powers neither realm is capable of comprehending nor controlling. Aside from that, adversaries may target them for exploitation or destruction."

Dahlia's expression remained unwavering as she argued, "This pregnancy could push Domiel over the edge. We need to carefully examine the situation."

"Negative repercussions follow reckless actions, Azrael. You should not have surrendered to your desires," Jahoel reprimanded. "Angels should always exercise restraint and wisdom in their actions. A relationship of this nature without considering the ramifications shows little foresight on your part. I'm not just referring to you and Annalise; it's about the balance between our worlds."

"You presume to lecture me about restraint and wisdom?" I retorted as my anger rose. "And you haven't engaged in promiscuous behavior? Besides, something much deeper than mere lust binds Annalise and me. She is my eternal soulmate, whom I love deeply. After all, Father sent her to me."

"Calm down, both of you," Dahlia said, pushing us apart. "Father has always planned for everything, but this seems unexpected. Maybe these children are His way of implementing His plan to bring angels and humans together. There is a possibility that your children will be the bridge between our worlds."

Annalise quickly approached us. "What's going on here?" she asked, her gaze moving between us. "You can feel the tension from across the room. Even Theo and Willow noticed it."

Heaving a sigh, I waved my hand in the air. "Nonsense, that's what."

"It's not nonsense," Jahoel assured her. "If your babies are angel-human hybrids, we need to understand the implications," Jahoel continued, his tone sharp. "For their safety and ours, it is crucial to address this now since their powers might be unpredictable. We can't ignore something this significant."

"Does he have a point?" she asked, looking at me, her hands shaking as she spoke. "Should we be concerned?"

Before answering, I replayed Father's conversation in my head, trying to recall any hint of worry in His voice. If there was a reason to warn us, He would have done so. Though Jahoel's concern seemed unwarranted, his instincts were never wrong. My gaze shifted to Theo and Willow, who stared at us and whispered. Ultimately, I decided to follow my instincts. "If there was cause for concern, Father would have said something. He didn't, so we should trust Him."

"It doesn't mean we shouldn't be vigilant," Jahoel emphasized.

"Yes, but let's first consult with Father before making any assumptions," I replied.

Annalise took a breath and nodded nervously. "I think that's a valid point."

The doorbell rang, and chimes filled the house. Before I could answer the door, Theo pulled it open. Father stood on the porch carrying a black briefcase. He smiled at Theo, saying, "Hello, young Theo. May I come in? I'm here to see Azrael."

"Did you mean Clay?" Theo asked, bringing his eyebrows together.

Laughing softly, Father said, "Oh, yes, Clay."

"Are you God?" Theo asked curiously, as if he had encountered a superhero from a favorite storybook.

Willow clutched Theo's hand and whispered, "He doesn't look like the pictures."

"Well," Father chuckled, "pictures sometimes only capture a glimpse of who we truly are." He stepped inside and stooped down to their level. In a lighthearted tone, He added, "But today, I'm just a regular dad visiting my sons and daughter." He gave Theo's shoulder a gentle squeeze and nodded warmly at Willow before heading over to Jahoel, Dahlia, and me.

His eyes shone with affection as He kissed Dahlia and Jahoel on each cheek. "My dear children," He said, hugging them both tightly. "It's wonderful to see you again."

When He approached me, His arms lingered around me a moment longer than the others. His touch carried a level of emotion reserved just for me, and it was a strong and comforting embrace that I would cherish forever. "Azrael, I'm delighted you're home." As He pulled away, His gaze met mine and He asked, "How are you feeling?"

"Much better, Father," I replied, feeling His love envelope me.

"I'm glad to hear that, Son. Remember, no matter what challenges you face, you have the strength and wisdom to overcome them," He said, His voice resonating with confidence. As He held up the briefcase, He gestured toward the dining room. "I brought gifts. Let's sit down and talk."

Pointing at myself, I asked, "Just me or everyone?"

"You and Annalise," He replied.

"Father, we must discuss the unborn twins," Jahoel urged. "There may be unforeseen challenges due to their unique lineage," he pressed, slightly on edge. "Their powers may be beyond our comprehension, and we should consider how celestial and earthly realms will react to their existence."

Father stared sternly at Jahoel and replied, "Let me talk to Annalise and Azrael about other matters before we talk about the twins."

Dahlia tucked her arm under Jahoel's, leading him toward Theo and Willow. "We'll keep the children busy while you talk."

"Thank you, Dahlia."

Annalise and I led Father into our dining room. A large oak table dominated the middle, surrounded by plush, high-backed chairs. Abstract art graced the walls, and large windows let natural light flood the room. A vase in the center of the table, filled with fresh flowers, scented the air. Laughter and conversation from the other room provided a comforting background hum for our conversation to begin.

Father sat across the table from us and set the briefcase on top of the table. As He unfastened the brass clasps, He revealed a rich burgundy interior that stood out against the dark case. Father carefully spread its contents on the table, unveiling a variety of legal documents.

"My angelic team has created your identity documents and vital records. Azrael, I have a Social Security card for you as Clay Bennett and one for Annalise as Annalise Bennett. I have four passports if you decide to travel as a family." He passed them out like a deck of cards. "I also have driver's licenses for Clay Bennett and Annalise Bennett." He thumbed through the stacks of papers as He continued. "I have a birth certificate for Clay Bennett and copies of original birth certificates for Annalise, Theo, and Willow."

Annalise stared at the documents laying out on the table. As our new beginning unfolded, she sucked in a breath and hovered her fingers uncertainly over the documents. I placed my hand over hers, and she turned to me and laughed nervously. "This is a lot to absorb."

"Yes, it is," I replied, meeting her gaze. "But we'll tackle this new chapter together, one step at a time."

Father's furrowed brow indicated an even greater concern about the next document. As He handed over the marriage certificate, His expression softened. "I know this may seem unconventional, but it ensured everything was in order for the adoption."

"Marriage certificate?" I blurted out. Given our eternal bond, I never considered marriage. She was my immortal partner, whom I adored immensely and could never live without. A ceremony or vows could not deepen the connection we already shared. Although I hadn't anticipated it, the prospect of formalizing our union in the human realm piqued my curiosity.

The elegant script and official seal drew Annalise's attention. She suppressed a giggle as she recognized my astonishment over the certificate. "It's just a formality in the human world," she assured me. "Our bond will never fade. No ceremony can change that."

Father smiled broadly and announced, "And here are Theo's and Willow's adoption papers. They have become part of your family."

Assuring Willow's and Theo's consent beforehand made the adoption papers that much more meaningful.

"We'll have to frame these and surprise them," Annalise said with tears in her eyes.

As Annalise wept on my shoulder, I choked back my own tears. The thought of providing stability for Theo and Willow after the tragedy of their father's death filled me with peace. I was determined to give them the best life. Together, we would heal and build a new future, honoring the memory of their father while creating our own path forward.

Father rested His hands on the armrest and inquired, "Do either of you have any questions about these documents?" His gaze shifted from us to the family room, suggesting He was ready to speak with Jahoel.

Seeing Annalise shake her head no, I turned back to Father and said, "No questions. I'll put them in the safe. Would you like me to tell Jahoel and Dahlia that we're ready?"

"Yes, please."

I rose from my seat, and Annalise followed suit. "I'll let them know," she said. "I want to ensure that Theo and Willow are preoccupied. It isn't necessary for them to hear this conversation." Her tone was firm, leaving no room for argument. Her eyes caught mine as she turned to leave, conveying a silent promise to protect them.

"I agree, Annalise," I said, gathering the documents.

Father nodded as well. "I think it's for the best."

We kept our important documents in a wall safe in our bedroom. Trying to hurry up, I stuffed everything inside, except for our driver's licenses, which I left on the dresser. Later, we could add them to our wallets. I hurried back into the dining room, not knowing where the conversation would lead.

Upon my return, I found Jahoel pacing anxiously, clearly preoccupied with his concerns about the twins. Dahlia sat calmly on one side of the table, her eyes following Jahoel's every move. Annalise sat in a chair on the other side, expressionless.

I slid into a chair next to her and whispered, "Where are Theo and Willow?"

"They're assembling a large puzzle in Theo's bedroom," she whispered back.

After kissing her cheek, I turned my attention to the conversation.

Jahoel paused mid-stride and asked Father, "Are these twins angel-human hybrids? If so, it's imperative to understand the implications for their safety and ours. Not to mention Domiel and other angels, who oppose any interaction between angels and humans."

"Jahoel," Father began, His voice relaxed yet authoritative. "The twins carry both angelic grace and human spirit, a rare and delicate balance. Their lineage is indeed unique, but they are under my protection, and I will handle Domiel or anyone else who threatens their existence."

"What do you mean by your protection?" Jahoel asked. "Are you responsible for creating these twins?"

"Jahoel!" Dahlia exclaimed.

"It's okay, Dahlia," Father replied calmly.

As I grasped Annalise's hand, my gaze landed on hers. Was she wondering the same thing I was—why did they need protection, and did my Father manipulate their conception?

Father continued, "Jahoel deserves an answer to his question. Azrael and Annalise conceived these twins, not me. I did not play any part in their conception or development. However, I am glad to know that they will serve as symbols of harmony between angels and humans. My statement emphasizes the importance of protecting the twins from Domiel and other adversaries."

Dahlia's lips parted as she blinked. After a brief pause, she composed herself. "I also stated that these children would bridge our worlds."

"You are very wise, Dahlia."

"Thank you, Father," Dahlia replied, blushing a little.

As Jahoel continued his rant, he taunted, "I mean no disrespect to you, Father, but isn't it a coincidence that these twins coincide with your plans to unite angels and humans on Earth? I find it difficult to believe that such a significant event could happen purely by chance," he continued, his eyes narrowing with suspicion. "It seems their conception aligned perfectly with your vision, Father."

As Dahlia leapt up from her chair, she shouted, "Jahoel, what is wrong with you?" She lowered her voice and then proceeded. "With his relentless theories, Domiel has always questioned Father's plans. You, Jahoel, have never doubted His divine wisdom, which guides us. You sound like Domiel now. What's going on?"

The tension in the room intensified with every word exchanged between Jahoel, Dahlia, and Father. Annalise scooted closer to me, her gaze bouncing between the three of them. The conversation was awkward and uncomfortable for both of us. I didn't know if I should intervene or remain silent. Raising angel-human children was an unknown. I didn't know what to expect, but there were definitely challenges they would face in a world not prepared for their dual nature. These were my own fears, but I sensed they were Father's, Dahlia's, certainly Jahoel's, and possibly Annalise's too.

In His gentle, soothing voice, Father assured Dahlia, "We should always have open discussions and allow different perspectives to coexist. We strengthen our bond and deepen our awareness when we share our thoughts and doubts with each other." Father glanced at Jahoel as He said, "True insight comes from understanding all sides of a situation."

Dahlia bowed her head and said, "You're right, Father."

As Jahoel stood silently, his arms folded and he gazed at the floor.

Father turned His attention to Annalise and me. "Here we are talking about your children as if you aren't even in the room. I do apologize. Do either of you have any concerns or questions about their upbringing or the challenges involved with raising hybrids?"

"I'm overwhelmed," Annalise replied in a small voice. "I didn't realize that being pregnant would cause conflict with others. The birth of a baby should bring joy, not gloom. Everyone talks about the heavy burden and responsibility my children will face. My hope is that they will grow up as normal children."

As I listened to her, my emotions surged: guilt for the burden our lineage imposed upon our unborn children, fear for the uncertain future they would face, and determination and readiness to shield them. The prospect that our children's lives would be anything but normal made me feel anxious and that I was to blame.

Father explained to us, "Your children will sense when it is time to develop their angelic qualities."

Annalise furrowed her brows, and a confused glaze filled her eyes as she asked, "Are you saying that at some point my children and I will be separated?"

"I apologize for not making myself clear. They will always be your children. Their purpose will merely shift," Father clarified.

Her anxious expression ripped my heart open. She had trusted me, but now she was uncertain and anxious. I wish I had been able to ease her distress somehow, but all I could do was say, "I am sorry."

Taking my face in her palms and kissing me, she said, "Don't apologize, Clay. I love you. No one is to blame. Together, we will make this work for the benefit of our extraordinary children."

"I don't know what I did to deserve you," I whispered as I hugged her.

Holding me tight, she said, "It's your love that gives me hope, even in moments of uncertainty."

"Welcome to our celestial family," Jahoel sarcastically blurted, slumping into a chair and shaking his head. "Where every decision is weighed against the fate of the world—and for you, making sure your children don't accidentally start the apocalypse."

As Dahlia rested her hand on Annalise's shoulder, she smiled. "Ignore him. He's being dramatic." With genuine love in her voice, she continued, "I'm thrilled to become an aunt. The twins' arrival will brighten our lives. Though Jahoel protests now, trust me, he'll spoil them with toys and stories of old."

"We will nurture their unique gifts with love, guidance, and warmth as we embrace their future together," Father said, echoing Dahlia's words.

While sitting quietly next to her, I noticed Annalise's hands trembling. I was almost ready to take hold of her hands, but as she listened to Dahlia and my Father, her trembling stopped, and she relaxed a little. Knowing that my family loved her made my heart grow warm.

Chapter 13

I snuggled up by the fireplace with Annalise after everyone had left and Theo and Willow had gone to bed. With their hypnotic colors, the orange, red, and yellow flames danced before us, soothing the day's events. Creating a tranquil atmosphere, the flickering fire cast gentle shadows on the walls. As we sipped hot cocoa, the rich chocolate flavor mingled with the scent of pine, and the gentle crackling of the logs added a comforting soundtrack.

"This is nice," Annalise murmured as she cuddled closer to me. Her head rested against my shoulder as she let out a contented sigh. She turned her face slightly toward me, her eyes half-closed in bliss, and she whispered, "I could stay like this forever."

My lips softly touched hers as I leaned forward to kiss her. Her soft and fragrant hair brushed against my cheek as I pulled her closer, intensifying our intimacy. In each other's presence, the world outside faded away, leaving only the two of us and the cozy warmth of the fire.

Alan's voice filled my head. "Clay, I'm ready. Come quickly. I can't go through this alone." I pulled away from Annalise, my gaze drifting away. I was no longer Death, but how could I abandon Alan? I would never have approached Annalise and confessed my love for her without his constant interference. Alan's plea reminded me of the role I once played, and the responsibility to free his soul tugged at my conscience. As much as I wanted to stay cocooned in Annalise's warmth and comfort, I owed it to him to be by his side now, especially when he needed Death most.

As Annalise watched me, her eyebrows came together, and she gently squeezed my hand. In a soft voice, she asked, "Is everything all right?"

"Alan's time has come, and he's begging me to come to him." Remorse laced my words. "I can't ignore him. We've spent countless hours by his side, delaying the inevitable, and now it's time to let him find peace."

"You should go to him," Annalise urged. "He needs you."

"I'll inform Dahlia and Jahoel. I trust them to keep everyone safe, but I need them to be extra cautious as Domiel remains unpredictable," I continued but kept my voice calm. "As soon as I can, I will return, but until then we must remain vigilant."

****

After ringing the doorbell, I waited outside Alan's mansion. A member of his staff opened the door several minutes later. He had on a well-tailored suit, his hair neatly combed as he stood tall. Nodding in acknowledgement, he asked, "Are you Clay?"

"Yes, I am."

"Mr. Hawk is expecting you," he said, stepping aside to let me in. We passed the exquisite artwork in the foyer before heading up the walnut staircase. On the second floor, ornate sconces cast a warm glow, illuminating a long hallway. The richly patterned rugs muffled our footsteps as we traveled down the corridor. My gaze swept the hallway as I observed a collection of awe-inspiring paintings, each more captivating than the previous.

His pace slowed as he approached the last of three doors. After opening the door, he escorted me inside. In the past, it might have been a bedroom, but now it resembled a hospital room. Alan lay in a hospital bed surrounded by pillows and blankets while state-of-the-art medical equipment displaying his vital signs beeped in the background. An IV stand stood next to the bed; its clear tubing disappeared into the vein in his arm, supplying him with some sort of medication. Moonlight, filtering through a small opening between the thick drapes covering the large windows, illuminated the clinical environment.

"Clay has arrived, sir," the man announced before closing the door behind him and leaving Alan and me alone.

Looking at Alan's frail figure, a stark contrast to the once vibrant man, my heart ached. His eyes were now dull and sunken, and his skin was grayish in color. I wasn't sure if he was even coherent since he seemed to stare straight through me. As I took a deep breath, I prepared to offer him comfort and strength.

At that moment, he blurted out, "Clay?"

I sat down in a chair by his bedside and gently grasped his hand, feeling his cool skin against mine. "Yes, Alan. It's me, Clay," I replied.

A faint smile touched his lips, and his eyes flickered with recognition. "Jeans, an untucked shirt, and tousled hair? That's a whole new you. Does this mean what I think it means?" He asked, his hand trembling as he waved a finger at me.

I grinned broadly. "What do you think it means?"

"Did Annalise bring about this change in you? Have you two finally started a relationship?"

My eyes crinkled with laughter. "We're finally together, and we've adopted two children, Theo, 10, and Willow, 9, and Annalise is expecting twins!"

"Whoa, and Annalise? How is she doing?" Alan asked.

My heart pounded at the thought of Annalise. "She's amazing, and I'm in awe of her," I said, my affection evident. "She is so kind to the children, but we're both a little overwhelmed about expanding our family so quickly." My thoughts shifted to Domiel. "One of my brothers opposes the bond between angels and humans, so we've had to contend with him as well. Enough about me. I'm here to help you."

His eyebrows lifted subtly, and I could see the gears turning in his mind as he processed the news. Despite his frailty, curiosity flickered across his features. "That's quite a change, Clay. How does being a family man fit into the whole Angel of Death thing?"

"My Father is looking for suitable replacements to take on this responsibility."

His breath caught in his throat. "Your Father, as in…"

A chuckle escaped my lips as Alan's eyes widened in disbelief. "Yes, my Father is God."

An amused glint flashed in his gaze as he murmured, "That explains a lot." He blinked. "But wait. I'm dying, and you're here."

"It had to be me who sent you to the afterlife, not a stranger. But I have more news to share. I've always had a strong desire to assist others, not merely guide them on their journey. My Father recognized this and declared me an angel of mercy." My gaze lingered on his before I continued. "So, Alan, I offer you two choices. The afterlife awaits you or I can heal your heart."

"What have I done to deserve this?" Alan spoke in a barely audible voice. "I can't believe this is happening. Can I really have a second chance?" Alan's expression revealed his internal struggle between accepting life or accepting death.

Seeing the conflict on his face and knowing the magnitude of the choice before him, my heart beat with empathy as I nodded.

"Even if I choose to live, I won't live forever. I'm human. We all have a time clock. Death is inevitable. When that time comes, I do not know how I will deal with it a second time. I have led a long, fulfilling, and enjoyable life." He paused, his gaze flicking upward. Looking back at me, he shook his head. "No, Clay. It's time for me to depart this world."

"Very well, Alan," I replied in Death's kind and compassionate voice. I gently placed my hand on his shoulder, feeling the warmth of his spirit still clinging to his frail body. "You've made a brave choice," I said softly. As I prepared to guide him on his final journey, tranquility enveloped the room, and Alan's lips curled into a peaceful smile.

Chapter 14

Just before dawn, I began my morning run. As the sun rose, it cast a golden hue over the quiet suburban streets. The air was crisp and fresh, and a hint of dew still covered the grass. My mind wandered as the sound of my feet striking the pavement echoed in my ears. Annalise's swollen belly was a sign that our twins were two weeks late. As she joked about not being able to see her toes, I think I was the one who was more nervous. I hoped that love and determination would guide me as I became a parent. Willow and Theo, my adorable humans, gave me plenty of practice. My heart swelled with pride every time they called me "Dad," and I teared up every time they called Annalise "Mom." Both Willow's wildflower-themed room and Theo's music-themed room proudly displayed their framed adoption papers. Becoming a father that day would always hold a special place in my heart.

Theo's and Willow's excitement about the twins' arrival was heartwarming. They helped in every way possible, making Annalise her tea, accompanying me to the grocery store, assisting with cooking, loading the dishwasher, cleaning the house, and even doing some laundry. Theo practiced lullabies on his mini guitar, eager to serenade the twins to sleep. On the other hand, Willow began drawing, decorating the nursery walls with colorful pictures.

I could handle a 10-year-old and a 9-year-old, but babies were intimidating. My mind visualized them crying and me wondering why. I imagined the sleepless nights ahead, pacing the nursery to calm them down. I worried about changing diapers, bath time, and their constant need for attention. Even despite my fears, I couldn't wait to hold them in my arms for the first time.

We rarely mentioned Domiel's name anymore. Father's mentorship and channeling Domiel's anger appeared to work. While the fear and anxiety about Domiel's threats had faded, I was not ready to let him back into our lives. As a husband and father, I had to protect my family.

By the time I reached our street, I was sweating profusely. My pace quickened as soon as I spotted the addition's roofline. After a grueling six months, Dahlia and Jahoel finally had their own space, with Theo and Willow constantly visiting them. Having the kids surrounded by happiness and security after such tragedy was more than I could ask for.

In the final block, I sprinted, reaching our driveway in seconds. Stretching my body, I breathed deeply, grateful for the way the run cleared my mind and revitalized me. The cool morning breeze brushed against my skin, a welcome contrast to the heat of my exertion. The tension in my muscles eased, leaving me calm and ready to face the day ahead.

As I opened the front door, Willow's high-pitched giggles mixed with Theo's infectious laughter echoed throughout the entryway. I followed the joyful noise into the kitchen, where I froze. Flour covered them, and the white powder littered the counters, the stove, and the floor. A trail of flour footprints led from the pantry to the island, where the two stood with mischievous grins. On the countertop, a wooden spoon poked out from beneath a toppled mixing bowl and a mound of flour. Nearby, a half-cracked egg dripped slowly off the edge, forming a small, sticky puddle on the floor.

"It looks like a bakery exploded here," I said, shaking my head in exasperation as I surveyed the chaotic scene.

With her face smeared with flour, Willow proudly held up a whisk. "We're making pancakes."

I chuckled as I wiped the flour off their faces. "I can't decide whether to call it culinary creativity or a kitchen catastrophe, but you've certainly left your mark."

A chorus of giggling erupted as Theo and Willow exchanged triumphant high-fives. "It's definitely art," Theo insisted.

"We're the artists!" Willow exclaimed with pride.

Gesturing around the kitchen with my finger, I said, "Hopefully, some pancakes make it to the griddle while I grab a quick shower." As I headed toward the bedroom, I couldn't help but smile as they whispered and plotted their pancake masterpiece.

When I opened our bedroom door, Annalise had just finished making the bed and placing the accent pillows on the comforter. She wore her hair back in a loose bun, accentuating her beauty. Bright morning light filtered through the window, casting a warm glow over the neatly arranged room. She glanced at me and asked, "How's the pancake project coming along?"

"The kitchen has been rebranded in flour and egg," I replied, leaning in to kiss her. "I hope you're ready for a breakfast that's as experimental as it is creative."

"I sure am," she said with a wink.

"Gonna grab a quick shower." I pointed to my clothes. "I'm all sweaty."

"You must have taken quite a run this morning," she teased, wrinkling her nose playfully. "I could smell the evidence the moment you walked in."

Before closing the bathroom door behind me, I said, "Ha, ha. Very funny."

My eyes closed as the hot water enveloped me like a comforting embrace. As my body relaxed, I inhaled the steam. What mattered was the soothing rhythm of the water raining on me and the warmth of the steam. The heat and peacefulness were too appealing, so I lingered in the shower longer than normal. After reluctantly turning off the water, I wrapped myself in a towel and left the bathroom. Having towel dried my hair, I dressed in joggers and a T-shirt in front of the mirror. The memory of admiring my perfectly groomed hair and Armani suit in the mirror at the French Quarter hotel made me laugh wholeheartedly.

My damp hair fell in messy waves, a stark contrast to the sleek style I once meticulously maintained, and my casual, laid-back clothes were a far cry from the polished persona I once projected. Despite the differences, I found this relaxed version of myself satisfying. Annalise had changed me for the better. I felt a profound sense of satisfaction as I took in the quiet sanctuary of the bedroom. The difference between the person I was and the person I became was obvious: Annalise had walked into my life.

As Willow's shrill scream pierced my ears, a wave of panic ripped through my spine and pinched the skin on the back of my neck. Her cry came from Jahoel and Dahila's suite. With adrenaline coursing through my veins, I bolted upstairs, my heart racing and my feet barely touching the ground. The image of Willow in danger flooded my mind, and I couldn't shake the fear. Was she injured? Was it Jahoel or Dahila who sustained an injury? The urgency of the situation left no room for hesitation.

A few seconds after I reached their closed door, Annalise and Theo ran up the stairs. I stopped them by holding up my hand. Cracking the door slowly, I peered inside and breathed in the metallic odor of blood. Domiel stood over Jahoel's and Dahlia's bodies, his gaze wild and intense. He clutched two golden daggers in his fists and tied several more to the belt around his waist. The blades glistened in the light, their edges razor-sharp, at least 12 inches long. Malevolent, dark, vein-like lines seemed to pulse through the gold metal as if alive.

Jahoel and Dahlia lay still on the floor, golden daggers embedded in their chests. The carpet turned deep crimson as blood pooled around them. Dahlia's eyes were open, frozen in shock, while Jahoel's hand stretched out, reaching for something—or someone.

Silence hung in the air, interrupted only by Jahoel's and Dahlia's shallow, labored breathing. Willow stood just a few feet from the doorway, staring at Domiel. Fear paralyzed her, and her hands shook uncontrollably as tears streamed down her cheeks.

Domiel's gaze met mine as the half-opened door caught his attention. In a fit of rage, he hurled a golden dagger straight at me. The blade's edge skimmed past my face, just missing me. A frustrated growl echoed from his throat. Its reverberation rippled throughout the room, promising even greater violence. Over my shoulder, I glanced at Annalise and Theo. We exchanged terrified looks.

"Domiel," I shouted in an authoritative tone. "Stop this madness!"

As he reached for another dagger, it slipped out of his grasp and hit the floor. He grunted something unrecognizable as he bent down to pick it up. Seeing an opportunity, I seized it. "Run, Willow!" I commanded, frantically waving her forward.

Willow sprinted toward me, each step fueled by sheer terror. Her small frame trembled with fright as her eyes locked onto mine. My arms encircled her tightly as she slammed into me, her sobs shaking us both. After tucking her behind me, I guided her toward Annalise. Relief swept over Annalise's face as she held Willow in a protective embrace. It wasn't long before Theo joined in, wrapping his arms around Annalise and Willow.

"Annalise," I whispered, "get Willow and Theo out of the house."

"No. Not without you."

In haste, I shooed her away. "Now, Annalise."

Neither of us backed down. She continued to shake her head stubbornly as we stared at each other.

"Go," I urged.

She grabbed Willow's and Theo's hands and glanced at me once more with tears streaming down her face.

"Stop!" Domiel yelled as he plowed through the door, knocking me over.

A cold sweat oozed from my pores as I scrambled backward, shielding my family with my body. The fierce love I had for Annalise, Willow, and Theo fueled me to be strong for them. I couldn't falter, not now. I had to protect them at all costs, and failure was not an option.

"No one leaves this house!" Domiel hissed, spitting out his words. Pointing a rigid finger at Annalise, he yelled, "Especially her!"

The room seemed to shrink as Domiel's shadow stretched ominously across the floor. He gazed at me with a deadly intensity, and his voice dripped with malice. I stood my ground, refusing to let him see my fear. Annalise clutched Willow and Theo as she drew closer to me. I kept my gaze on Domiel, not letting him escape my sight. In a surrendering gesture, I held up my hands, hoping to appease him. "Calm down. What do you want?"

He fingered a dagger handle. Was he thinking of throwing it? With a bellowing voice, he proclaimed, "Those twins cannot be born. Their creation is an abomination to all angels."

The thought of my twins dying before they were able to live filled me with desperation. Behind me, Annalise trembled in response to Domiel's dark threat. Her fear entwined itself with mine, a persistent reminder that I could not fail.

"Don't touch her," Theo warned with defiance, his small frame shuddering behind me.

I glanced at Theo and shook my head. "Theo, let me handle this." As I turned back around, I caught movement behind Domiel. Jahoel managed to stand up despite his injuries. I clamped my lips together to silence a gasp. Blood soaked through Jahoel's shirt around the dagger lodged in his chest. Slowly, he progressed forward, grimacing with each step. He reached for the dagger's hilt buried inside his chest as he neared Domiel. Did he plan to stab Domiel with the very dagger that had wounded him?

To buy Jahoel the time he needed, I raised my voice, hoping to drown out any sound. "Why do you say this about my twins? What do you know that Father does not?"

Domiel's face contorted as he ground out his words. "We are superior beings, created to serve a higher purpose. Humans are flawed, fragile, and incapable of understanding divine complexity. This hybrid species is a dangerous experiment that may result in mutations, abnormalities, and even death."

While keeping my eyes on Jahoel, I calmly replied, "You have no proof, and you're speculating. Father would never allow their conception if any of that were possible."

"I don't need proof," Domiel spat. "If hybrids were meant to exist, they'd have been created centuries ago."

Seeing the dagger's edge sparkle in Jahoel's hand, I took a step back. Jahoel thrust the blade downward, stabbing Domiel between the shoulders. With a thud, the fallen angel's body crumpled to the ground. Domiel lay still, his limbs awkwardly splayed. As Jahoel stood over him, his expression was devoid of emotion.

I gathered Annalise, Willow, and Theo and pushed them forward as we raced down the stairs. Jahoel's grim actions startled me, but morality was irrelevant to me at that moment, and he had neutralized Domiel's threat, helping me protect my family.

As we approached the doorway, a blinding burst of light blocked our path. As the ethereal glow faded, a woman emerged. I recognized her pale blue eyes and dark, flowing hair instantly. My mother touched my shoulder and said, "I'm here, son."

With a sharp intake of breath, I exclaimed, "Domiel is back! He attacked Dahlia and Jahoel, stabbing them with golden daggers. I believe the blades were poisoned, just like the chains he used on me. Jahoel managed to get up and go after him, but now they're all in the suite upstairs... lifeless. I think the poison—" I couldn't finish the sentence. They had to be safe. I had to believe that. "When will this madness end, Mother?" My gaze shifted to Annalise, Willow, and Theo. "Look at them. They're terrified."

She embraced them and apologized with sincerity. "I'm so sorry. Words aren't enough." She released them and faced me, admitting, "Domiel played on your Father's sympathy. He plotted revenge even as we thought the calming exercises had worked." Her eyes narrowed, and her voice was fierce. "And to answer your question, Azrael, it ends today. I will handle this. Wait here."

A supreme glow lit the blue hue of my mother's eyes as she held her head high and squared her shoulders. Her divine light surrounded her as she ascended the stairs. I knew her power allowed her to end this on her own, but my guilt consumed me. I should be at her side. Was this not also my burden? Shouldn't I be helping to resolve this nightmare? Dahlia and Jahoel had risked their lives to ensure our safety, and I had no idea what awaited my mother once she reached their room. Were they dead, still at war, or clinging to life?

My mother reached the second floor and disappeared down the hallway. I turned to Annalise; her arms were wrapped tightly around Willow and Theo as they clung to her, their gazes filled with horror.

"I should help my mother," I whispered into Annalise's ear.

Annalise grabbed my arm and pulled me closer to her and the children. "She told you to wait here. I understand that you feel responsible. I do too. This entire situation revolves around us, our relationship, and love for each other. Someone must put an end to Domiel's madness. I believe that person is your mother. More importantly, we need you here with us."

I nodded reluctantly. A part of me wanted to run after my mother to protect her from danger. My other instinct was to protect Annalise and the children. Duty and love tugged at my heart, but Annalise's words and Willow's and Theo's vulnerable gazes kept me anchored at their side. I wrapped my arms around all three of them in a caring embrace. As Annalise's hair brushed against my cheek, Willow and Theo clung to me. Holding them close, I promised, "Everything will be all right. It's finally over."

Willow's shoulders shook as she wept, her tears soaking my shirt. Theo, though scared, put on a brave face.

"Is it over, Clay?" Annalise asked, her eyes searching mine.

As I kissed her cheek, I let my lips linger against her soft skin and answered, "I promise it is."

Flashes of ethereal light lit up the staircase, followed by loud popping sounds that jogged my memories of the incident at the church. Throughout the house, the sharp crackling echoed like distant fireworks. Each ear-piercing blast coming from Dahlia and Jahoel's suite made me flinch. The shockwaves vibrated the entire house, causing the curtains to flutter and the windows to rattle.

"Not again!" Willow shrieked.

Annalise tightened her grip on my arm, her breath catching with every sound.

I was filled with thoughts of my mother facing Domiel alone. There were no human sounds coming from the suite—no voices, no screams, just the celestial fireworks. What was my mother up to? Despite my apprehension, I had to keep my promise to Annalise and the kids. I smoothed Willow's hair as I said, "We're safe, Willow. We can trust my mother."

As the brilliance and crackling faded, the room fell into silence, and an eerie calm replaced the commotion. Annalise and I exchanged worried glances. What did the silence mean—total destruction—death? Before more horrible thoughts filled my head, my mother appeared at the top of the stairs, alone. She hurried toward us, her gaze falling on Willow's and Theo's terrified expressions.

"Don't be afraid," she said in a soothing tone as she held them in her arms. "I have taken care of everything." After a moment, she released them and turned to Annalise and me. "The situation is grave. Though I destroyed the daggers and purged the poison from their bodies, the damage is already done." She closed her eyes and shook her head as if she were shaking away reality. "I sealed Dahlia, Jahoel, and Domiel in my celestial light and sent them to your Father."

Theo interrupted her and blurted out, "Are Dahlia and Jahoel dead?"

"No, Theo." Mother confirmed, exhaling with relief. "They are alive."

"When Domiel hurt Dad, Jahoel took him to the hospital," Willow pointed out in her small voice. "Maybe the doctors can fix Dahlia and Jahoel, too?"

As Mother bent down to Willow's level, she cupped her face in her hands. "What a kind thought, Willow. Doctors cannot treat Dahlia's and Jahoel's injuries with medicine or bandages due to the poison. It is for this reason that I sent them to Heaven. Their Father will heal them."

With a furrowed brow, Willow glanced at me. "Dad, did your Father heal you too?"

I hesitated, knowing the truth was beyond her grasp. How could I explain that my Father came to me in a vision and had drawn out the poison while I was under anesthesia? "Yes, Willow," I replied gently. "In a way, He did. My Father helped me feel better when I was very sick, just like He'll help Dahlia and Jahoel now. It's a special kind of healing that only He can do."

As she nodded slowly, the frown on her forehead vanished. "I hope they get well soon so they can come back home."

Annalise gasped and doubled over, clutching her stomach just as I was about to respond to Willow. I reached out instinctively, my hand resting on her back. "Annalise, what's wrong?"

Her eyes dulled as her face paled. She grabbed my arm and cried out. "I think I'm having contractions."

Contractions! My brain screamed, sending a shockwave of panic through me. Trying to keep my voice calm, I said, "We should head to the hospital. Let me grab my keys. Willow, could you bring me the hospital bag? It's in our bedroom closet on the floor."

With a nod, she ran up the stairs.

My heart pounded as I raced into the kitchen and snatched my keys off the island. After checking my jacket pocket for my wallet and phone, I headed back to Annalise. I watched her face contort in pain as she leaned against my mother. "Hang on, Annalise. We'll be at the hospital soon."

Willow returned with the hospital bag and Annalise's phone, handing both to me. As I laid the bag down, I turned to my mother and asked, "Can you stay with the kids?"

"Of course," Mother replied without hesitation. "I'll take care of things here. You concentrate on getting Annalise to the hospital safely."

I handed Annalise's phone to my mother. "I'll keep you updated on Annalise's phone. You do know how to use a cell phone, right?"

Mother stared at the phone for a second or two before glancing at me.

"I'll help her," Theo offered. He gave my mother a quick nod before running to Annalise. Both he and Willow hugged her tightly.

"I need you both to behave yourselves while I'm away at the hospital," Annalise said as she held them in her arms. "Help each other with chores, and if you disagree, talk it out calmly. I'll miss you both."

When Willow spoke, her voice quivered. "We promise, Annalise. We'll miss you."

Theo nodded in agreement, adding, "And we'll take care of each other."

"Don't worry, Annalise," my mother assured her. "I'll keep them busy with fun activities and make sure they keep to their schedule."

"Thank you," Annalise said between labored breaths.

As we headed out the door, I guided Annalise into the Hummer, my steady hands masking the anxiety clawing at my chest. I tossed the hospital bag on the back seat before calling Dr. Coffman to let her know we were on our way.

At every stoplight, my heart pounded as I maneuvered through traffic. Annalise gripped the seat tighter with each contraction. I could see her fingers turning white as she clutched the armrest, and her cries became louder. As she fought to focus on her breathing, she rattled off, "I didn't think the pain would be so intense."

"Keep breathing, Annalise," I urged. "We're almost there."

Reaching for her hand, I concentrated on the road, ensuring the safety of her and our babies. In less than 15 minutes, I pulled into the hospital parking lot. Since it was after hours, Dr. Coffman told me to meet her in the ER. Fortunately, the parking lot was nearly empty, allowing me to secure a spot close to the entrance. Annalise couldn't manage two steps, let alone two blocks. I lifted her from the Hummer and carried her into the building. As I rushed through the double doors, I shouted, "My wife is in labor! Dr. Coffman told us to meet her here."

My shout sent several nurses rushing toward us. They swept Annalise into a wheelchair and hurried us to a triage room, where a flurry of medical staff descended upon her. Nurses swapped her clothes for a gown, scrambled to attach monitors, and immediately checked her vitals and tracked the twins' heartbeats.

Looking at the monitor, one nurse asked, "When did your contractions start?"

"About twenty minutes ago," Annalise replied.

"How frequent are they?"

Annalise's pained expression said it all when she muttered, "Every few minutes, and they're getting worse and lasting longer."

The nurse entered the information into a laptop and assured Annalise, "You're doing great; just breathe through them."

Dr. Coffman entered the room at that moment. "Hello, Annalise, Clay." She greeted us with a kind smile. "Let's see how you and your babies are doing and how far along your labor has progressed." She had Annalise lie back on the table and draped a sheet over her legs for privacy. As Dr. Coffman snapped on sterile gloves, she explained, "I'm going to perform a pelvic exam to check your dilation and effacement." After a quick assessment, she glanced at the nurses with a sharp nod. "She's at ten centimeters and one hundred percent effaced. The water has broken." Dr. Coffman turned to us. "These babies are coming now. We're moving to the delivery room. There's no time for an epidural, but we'll start an IV for pain management immediately."

A nurse wheeled Annalise out of the triage room, down the hallway, and into the delivery room in a matter of seconds. The room was spacious, with pale blue walls that created a calming atmosphere. Bright overhead lights illuminated the medical equipment surrounding the hospital bed. The left corner of the room was filled with monitors and medical supplies, and two comfortable chairs sat next to the large window.

After Annalise settled into the bed, the nurse adjusted it into an upright position and instructed Annalise to move forward until her feet were on stirrups. The team worked quickly, securing her IV and the sterile drapes. Dr. Coffman took her spot at the foot of the bed and focused on Annalise. "Annalise, I will let you know when to push and when not to. Just breathe through each contraction."

Annalise nodded as I stood helpless by her bedside. As Death, I ended lives; I didn't create them. I didn't know what role I played— whether to speak or remain silent. I felt overwhelmed and unsure of how to help Annalise. In the process of pushing, Annalise clutched my hand tightly and groaned. I knew I should say something, but what? I whispered softly, "You're doing amazing, Annalise."

As her grip tightened on my hand, I squeezed back gently, hoping to convey my love and support.

Her face contorted as the next contraction hit.

"Keep pushing, Annalise," Dr. Coffman urged as she guided the birth.

Annalise leaned forward, groaning. Small beads of sweat appeared on her forehead, and her breathing came in short, focused bursts as she pushed with all her strength. Even though it was happening so fast, every second felt like an eternity. Raw emotion flooded my soul and escaped my lips as I gasped—the moment of birth etched into my memory. The baby let out a strong, healthy cry, and the room erupted in cheers.

"It's a boy!" Dr. Coffman exclaimed as Annalise experienced another contraction. "One more push, Annalise."

Annalise shuddered with exertion as she bore down again. I held onto her hand, squeezing it gently. "You're doing so well, Annalise," I said tenderly, brushing a damp strand of hair off her forehead. "Just a little more, and our babies will be in your arms."

After locking her eyes on mine, she gave a final, powerful push with a look of exhaustion on her face. A second cry filled the room, just as strong and powerful as the first. Annalise slumped back against the pillow, her eyes full of tears.

"A girl," Dr. Coffman said as she held the baby up for Annalise and me.

The nurses wrapped the twins in warm, soft blankets and placed them on Annalise's chest, their tiny fingers curling around hers. The girl had my pale blue eyes, while the boy had Annalise's sage green eyes. As I stroked their heads filled with dark hair, I murmured, "They're us reversed."

Softly laughing, she said, "I was thinking the same thing."

"You just went through the three stages of labor in record time," Dr. Coffman said, taken aback. "I've been doing this for many years," she added, "and it's not often I see such a smooth and quick delivery, especially for a first-time mother."

"I guess our little ones were just eager to meet us," Annalise replied, glancing down at the twins nestled against her chest. She gently squeezed my hand and then handed me our son. "He wants to meet you."

As I folded my arms around him, I glanced at Dr. Coffman and asked, "Am I doing this right?"

"You're doing great," she responded.

Annalise's eyes welled up with tears as she watched me cradle our son. His small body fit perfectly in the crook of my arm. As he snuggled closer and gazed up at me, a wave of awe washed over me. I stared down at this little being that I created with Annalise and realized that my life had forever changed. Rocking our baby boy back and forth in my arms, I asked, "I'm sure this is a silly question, but what happens next?"

A smile spread across Dr. Coffman's face. "We're here to help, and there truly are no silly questions. You and the twins will likely stay with us for the next twenty-four to forty-eight hours. While the nurses monitor the babies' vitals and handle their initial treatments, they'll also be looking after you—checking your recovery and helping you get started with breastfeeding."

"Is all that normal, or do we need to worry?" I asked as a knot formed in my stomach. The thought of anything going wrong with Annalise or the twins terrified me.

"Everything is fine," Dr. Coffman assured us. "Annalise and the twins are doing well. It's completely natural to feel anxious, but you can rest assured that we are here to support you throughout the process."

My stomach relaxed as did the tension in my jaw. "We're both new at this, and we can't thank you enough, Dr. Coffman."

"Of course. Being a new parent can be overwhelming, but you're doing great. You can ask all the questions you want."

As Annalise and I shared a moment, she reached up and touched my cheek. "Would you like to hold your daughter now?"

"Yes, I would love to," I replied, gently transferring our son to Annalise. As I cradled our daughter against my chest, she curled her fingers around my thumb. My heart gushed with affection. "We've been waiting for you," I said. It dawned on me at that moment that we hadn't decided on names. Domiel's relentless threats dominated our attention, and every conversation was about how we could protect our family. I laughed. "I think we should talk about names."

"Oh my gosh! There's been so much going on that I completely forgot."

"I did, too," I confessed, "but there's no better time than the present." Looking back and forth between our twins, I rattled off names that came to mind. "Ian and Ivy, Chloe and Christian, Zachary and Zoe, Luca and Lainey."

A sparkle of excitement lit Annalise's eyes. "Luca and Lainey. I love them."

I gave our daughter back to Annalise as I said, "I'm going to call my mother and update her." A broad smile spread across my face, and my voice rose with excitement. "She's going to be thrilled to hear about the little ones and their beautiful names."

Chapter 15

We arrived home two days later and were greeted with pink and blue balloons decorating the entrance, followed by various shades of pink and blue streamers hanging from the ceiling, leading us into the living room. A banner adorned the center wall that read, "Welcome Home, Luca and Lainey!" More balloons floated about the room with plush teddy bears and soft blankets arranged on the sofa.

Jahoel and Dahlia rested on the sofa amid the blankets and toys. I caught Jahoel wincing every time he moved and Dahlia leaning stiffly against the cushions. Settled on either side of them were Theo and Willow, holding baskets filled with colorful baby clothes, tiny shoes, rattles, and teething rings. My father stood by the fireplace with my mother at His side. My mother held two quilts—one for each twin—with names and birthdates embroidered on them.

As we entered, everyone quietly greeted us with, "Welcome home!"

"This is amazing," Annalise said, her smile illuminating the room.

I placed the infant carriers on the floor, and Theo and Willow rushed over and gently picked up the twins. Annalise's eyes glistened as Theo and Willow cooed and giggled at Luca and Lainey. Annalise smothered Theo and Willow with love, kissing both of them on the top of their heads and murmuring, "I missed you two."

"We missed you, too," Willow said, not taking her eyes off the twins.

I followed suit, kissing both of them on the cheek. "Be sure to support their heads like this," I said, gently adjusting Theo's and Willow's arms.

"I love them," Willow whispered, her eyes never leaving the twins.

"And I love their chubby cheeks," Theo added.

A laugh escaped me. I hadn't thought about it, but they were rather chubby.

"The twins love attention," Annalise gushed with a smile of pure bliss.

"How about watching the twins while Annalise and I greet the rest of the family?" I asked.

Willow and Theo enthusiastically agreed. "We can totally do it," Theo reassured me.

"Perfect. Remember to be careful," I advised.

"They will be fine," Annalise said, shooing me away.

We left Theo and Willow with the twins and approached Jahoel and Dahlia. I moved the toys and blankets to the far end of the sofa so Annalise and I could sit with them. We embraced them gently, but they hugged us passionately in return. When I pulled away, I asked, "How are you both feeling?"

"So, so," Jahoel said as he flipped his hand back and forth.

In a weak voice, Dahlia said, "Every day gets better."

Their suffering was evident in the creases on their brows. It pained me to bear witness to the torment they endured to protect my family. I gripped each of their shoulders as I said softly, "I am so sorry. Love surrounds you here."

"I hope you'll come back to stay with us soon, so we can take care of you as you did for us," Annalise offered as she squeezed their hands.

"Annalise is right. Your home is here with us, Theo, Willow, and the twins," I assured them, my voice resonating with sincerity.

A spark of life filled Dahlia's eyes as she looked at Annalise and me. "We love all of you."

"We will return soon," Jahoel promised. "We couldn't miss this joyous occasion—we had to be here for the twins."

I could see the pain in my brother's and sister's eyes and knew that more healing was required. Having been there, I knew how painful Domiel's wrath could be. It probably wasn't the right time, but I had to know what had happened. "And what about Domiel?" I asked in a low voice.

The two exchanged glances. Jahoel spoke. "He's healing too. However, there have been consequences to his actions."

"Consequences?"

Dahlia stated, "We cannot trust him. Measures were taken to prevent him from acting out again."

"What measures?" I asked. "What has happened?"

"Even after everything, he has learned nothing," Jahoel stated in a grim tone. "He refuses to let go of his vendetta against mankind. Hate has poisoned his heart and mind, making him untrustworthy, as Dahlia pointed out. Father had to make an extremely difficult decision to protect everyone. He stripped Domiel of his wings and hierarchy, forcing him to remain under watch in Heaven."

Upon discovering Domiel's decline, I experienced a wave of suffocating sorrow. I swayed and searched for balance before steadying myself. He had been the brother I looked up to, the brother I loved, and my best friend. I got that his actions had consequences; however, I was also conscious of the loss he must have been experiencing, knowing he once had a generous heart. I sadly shook my head and expressed quietly, "I hope one day he might find redemption and peace."

"Your hope for his redemption shows your compassion and love for him, Clay," Annalise said tenderly, placing her hand on my arm.

Dahlia waved us away from the sofa as she urged, "Don't let Domiel ruin this beautiful day. Say hello to Father and Mother. I know they are eager to express their congratulations."

Before leading Annalise away, I said, "We will never forget what you sacrificed to keep us safe. I love you both."

Once more, they waved us away, but not before I saw tears well up in their eyes.

As we approached my Father and Mother, I let go of any lingering thoughts about Domiel, instead focusing on the love and support that surrounded us. I embraced my parents warmly, eager to join them in celebrating this special occasion. "Father, Mother."

My mother presented Annalise and me with beautifully handcrafted quilts as she said, "Each thread is infused with blessings, weaving a tapestry of divine protection and love."

Annalise brushed her fingertips over the quilt as she gazed at it in awe. "It's exquisite," she murmured, tracing the intricate patterns with her fingertips. "Thank you. We will cherish them."

"They're beautiful, Mother," I said, kissing her cheek. "The twins will love them."

"We haven't had babies in our family in so long," she exclaimed, resting her hand over her heart.

Laughing joyfully, my Father agreed. "Too long. May we say hello to the twins?" He asked.

I gestured toward our twins. "Of course, please."

As my parents negotiated with Theo and Willow to hold our twins, Annalise and I stood together, watching them. In a very reluctant and almost tearful gesture, Theo and Willow handed my parents the twins. There was something so heartwarming about the scene. Annalise squeezed my hand, and we both smiled, feeling grateful for the love that surrounded us.

Annalise whispered to me, "I don't think we'll ever get our babies back."

"I believe you're right." My heart swelled with happiness, my giddiness nearly overflowing. As I basked in the bliss, memories of the day we met flooded back, transporting me to the Sip A Froth rooftop. As I had stared at her from across the table, she had asked if I was happy. At that time, happiness was not the purpose of my life. Since then, everything had changed. I had changed. Her warmth and spontaneity had softened my rigid outlook, opening my heart to new possibilities. Annalise showed me that happiness comes not from perfection or routine, but from the love, trust, and laughter we share every day.

"Clay?"

Annalise's voice shattered my thoughts. I turned to her and softly kissed her. When I pulled away, I asked, "Do you remember asking me if I was happy while we were sitting on the rooftop of *Sip A Froth*?"

Her sage-green eyes studied me intently. With a slight nod, she said, "I do. You said you knew your place and were comfortable with who you were. My next question was whether you were having a good time that day. You admitted you were."

"Annalise, you brought color into my world, laughter into silent moments, and love into my every heartbeat. You are my happiness, my anchor, and every day with you feels like the beginning of a beautiful new chapter. You are my everything, and I love you more than words can say."

Even with tears streaming down her cheeks, Annalise blushed with radiance. She reached up to touch my cheek. "You healed me and filled my life with joy I never dared dream of." Her voice quivered as she added, "I never knew a love like this was possible. Every moment together feels like a gift, and I cherish every laugh, every tear, and every heartbeat we share. I can't imagine my life without you."

Slowly and tenderly, I kissed her again, savoring her warm, soft lips. Words could never convey all the emotions I felt from that kiss. When we finally broke apart, our foreheads rested against each other, and I whispered, "Thank you for being my everything."

"Thank you for giving me everything I ever dreamed of."

"Well, at least we agree on being each other's everything."

We burst into laughter as we held onto each other. As I glanced at my family, I smiled. The twins were in my parents' arms, while Jahoel, Dahlia, Theo, and Willow sat on the sofa, the sheer look of contentment plastered on their faces. Looking back at Annalise, I asked, "Are you ready for our next chapter?"

Her gaze flicked from me to everyone on the sofa and then back to me. "I'm so ready."

About The Author

LAURA DALEO is a multi-genre author, specializing in dark fantasy, urban fantasy, supernatural fiction, science fiction, and young adult fiction. Immortal Kiss, her best-known vampire series, explores the Egyptian pantheon that gave rise to vampires. Currently, she is working on her ninth book, Wolf Experiment, an urban fantasy.

A native of San Diego, California, Laura now lives in Tucson, Arizona with her two dogs, Rose and Cooper.